D0188655

Blair's Nightmare

OTHER YEARLING BOOKS YOU WILL ENJOY:

YEARLING BOOKS/YOUNG YEARLINGS/YEARLING CLASSICS are designed especially to entertain and enlighten young people. Patricia Reilly Giff, consultant to this series, received her bachelor's degree from Marymount College and a master's degree in history from St. John's University. She holds a Professional Diploma in Reading and a Doctorate of Humane Letters from Hofstra University. She was a teacher and reading consultant for many years, and is the author of numerous books for young readers.

Blair's Nightmare

Zilpha Keatley Snyder

A YEARLING BOOK

Published by
Dell Publishing
a division of
Bantam Doubleday Dell Publishing Group, Inc.
666 Fifth Avenue
New York, New York 10103

The trademark Yearling® is registered in the U.S. Patent
and Trademark Office.

ISBN: 0-440-40915-2

Reprinted by arrangement with Atheneum Publishers

Printed in the United States of America

December 1985

10 9 8 7

CW

Blair's Nightmare

Chapter One

David had been dreaming that he was in the school cafeteria, and for a moment the noise fitted right in. In the dream he was carrying an enormous slippery tray full of food and looking for a place to sit down, but all the seats were full—except one. The one vacant chair was at a table where a bunch of guys stared at him and said things like, "Get lost," and "This seat is saved." He was trying to decide whether to remind Pete Garvey—the guy who said the seat was saved seemed to be Garvey—that seat-saving was against the rules, when there was this loud clatter and the guys at the table all laughed. David was thinking, Oh, no, and looking to see what had fallen off his tray, when suddenly there he was in bed. In bed and waking up and realizing that the scene in the cafeteria had been a dream. He was just lying there enjoying the flash of relief that comes when you wake up and realize a nightmare didn't really happen, when he became aware of a kind of echo in his ears. An echo that told him that part of it had been real. There really had been a bouncy clatter, and it had come from someplace not far away. From right there in the dark bedroom, in fact. That was when he sat up and turned on the light and found out that it was only Blair walking in his sleep again.

Blair had been walking in his sleep a lot lately. This time he must have been on his way to the window when he stumbled over his Randy the Robot toy, and it had been the robot bouncing around that woke David up. It didn't wake Blair up, though. People said it was dangerous to wake up a sleepwalker, but with Blair you didn't have to worry very much. Sleeping was one thing Blair did with a lot of determination, and waking him up wasn't about to happen by accident.

When the light went on, he went right on standing by the window. His pajama bottoms sagged in the rear and his curly hair looked as if it had been combed with an eggbeater. He was looking down into the side yard. At least, you would have thought he was looking if you didn't know about sleepwalkers. His eyes were wide open, but if he was seeing anything, it was probably only a scene from a dream. So David quietly led him back to bed. He was pulling up the covers when Blair sat up again and stared at David.

"David," he said.

David shook his head. According to Molly, David's stepmother, you were definitely not supposed to talk to sleepwalkers.

"David." Blair was pointing toward the window.

4

"Shhh," David said, pushing him back down.

Blair stared at him. "Shhh?" he asked. David nodded. After a moment Blair nodded, too, and lay back down. Even in his sleep Blair was pretty reasonable for a six year old.

It wasn't until morning that David found out what Blair had been dreaming about and what it was he thought he had looked at, down there in the empty moonlit yard. Blair told him all about it while they were getting dressed, and David immediately decided it would be a good idea to tell his father. Everybody knows that what people dream about is very significant and has a whole lot to do with their deep inner hopes and dreams and basic needs. And as it happened, Blair had been dreaming about a dog.

It was Saturday, a nice warm Saturday in late October, and everyone was having whole-grain waffles with fruit and yogurt for breakfast, except Amanda who hated health food.

Amanda, who was Molly's daughter and, of course, David's stepsister, had been the original health food nut in the family. But when Molly got interested, Amanda had decided the whole thing was a hoax and had switched to junk food. The result was some pretty complicated meals.

That morning Amanda kept pawing through the refrigerator and peering in the oven at the Pillsbury biscuits she was baking. Molly kept jumping up to check on the waffle iron. And, as usual, everyone was talking nonstop. Everybody except Blair, that is, who was, as usual, pretty silent. All the rest of the family, including Molly and Amanda, were great talkers, so meals were apt to be a kind of verbal soccer game, with everybody trying to steal the ball and run with it. If you wanted to be a part of the action you had to be pretty determined.

"Dad," David yelled at one point, over an argument about pantyhose between Molly and Amanda, and another one about who smeared jam all over the butter, between Janie and Esther. "Dad. We had a very interesting discussion in Social Studies the other day, about basic human needs. Did you study about basic needs when you were in school?"

"Basic needs?" Dad said. "You mean like food, clothing and shelter?"

"Yeah. Like that. And like social contact." David cupped one hand around his mouth and aimed what he was saying at Dad, over a chorus of you-did-toos and I-did-nots from Janie and Esther. "There was this part about social contact, about how baby monkeys need something warm and furry to hang onto while they're little, or they grow up to have weird personalities. And, Dad, Mr. Davenport said people are a lot like monkeys, and that's one reason why pets are important. Particularly pets that are warm and furry."

That hadn't been exactly the way Mr. Davenport had put it, but it was close. Close enough so that it had occurred to David at the time to wish his father could hear what Mr. Davenport was saying—because, although it was true that the Stanley family did have a few pets already, as Dad had pointed out, they didn't really have one of the warm and furry type. Like a dog, for instance.

"Warm and furry?" Dad looked very serious. "Warm and furry is all that important?" David was just wondering if he didn't look a little too serious, as if he were trying to keep from smiling, when Molly interrupted.

6

"Jeff, what do you think?" and she went on about how Amanda wanted to start wearing pantyhose to school and did Dad think pantyhose were necessary for someone who was barely fourteen. Before Dad could answer, Janie interrupted to ask everyone to look at her waffle.

"The jam on my waffle is obviously apricot," Janie said, "and if you will notice the mess on the butter, you will see that it is definitely boysenberry." Janie, who was eight years old and had an I.Q. of one hundred and forty-five, had recently decided she was a detective. "And now," she went on pointing at Esther, "may I direct your attention to Esther's chin."

Everybody looked. Esther stuck out her tongue and licked off the evidence.

"Apricot," she said, smacking her lips.

"It was not," Janie yelled.

"It was—" Esther started to yell, before Dad's stare got through to her, "—too," she whispered.

"It was not," Janie whispered back.

"It was too."

"It was not." The whispering got softer as Dad's glare got fiercer, until they were only mouthing the words at each other. Dad went back to eating his waffle, but it was obvious that he definitely wasn't in one of his better moods. David decided not to try again until everyone had finished eating and Janie and the twins had gone out to play. By then David and Amanda had started in on their Saturday morning dishwashing job, and Dad and Molly were having a last cup of coffee at the kitchen table. This time David decided on a different approach.

"It happened again last night," he said and waited for someone to say "What did?"—and right on cue, Molly said it. Considering all the publicity about lousy stepmothers, Molly could have been a lot worse. She wasn't a typical stepmother —or mother, either, for that matter. She was pretty small and young-looking for her age, which was thirty-six, and she went around wearing jeans and bare feet and paint-smeared smocks a lot of the time. She was a very good artist, but she wasn't exactly the greatest at things like housekeeping or cooking. She also tended to be more or less of a pushover. When you needed someone to set one up for you, Molly usually came through.

"What happened?" Molly said.

"Blair walked in his sleep again," David said.

"Again?" Molly looked anxious. "Jeff, I don't like it. It just doesn't seem normal for a five year old to suddenly start walking in his sleep all the time."

"Six. He's six, Molly. And I don't know if I'd call it 'all the time,'" Dad said. "This is the second time isn't it?"

"The third time that we know about. And there could have been other times, when he got back into bed by himself and no one noticed. It really worries me, Jeff. He could fall down the stairs, or even out of a window."

"Yeah," David said. "I woke up this time, but I might not always."

"You know," Molly said, "it just started since school began. I wonder if it could be related to school."

Dad grinned. "To first grade? I shouldn't think first grade could be all that stressful."

"Well no," Molly said, "not ordinarily. But you know, I

have some misgivings about Blair in that particular class."

David had heard Molly on that subject before. About how Mrs. Bowen, the first-grade teacher at Steven's Corners Elementary School, wasn't the right type of person to appreciate someone like Blair. David was inclined to agree about that. Blair was a pretty spacy kid, and Mrs. Bowen looked about as unspacy as you could get. But at the moment Molly's "school problems theory" was getting the conversation off on the wrong track.

"Blair dreams while he's sleepwalking," David said quickly. "I know because I asked him. You know what he dreams about, Dad? He dreams about a dog. You know, I'll bet Blair would stop sleepwalking if he had a dog."

"I see," Dad said. "A dog, is it? A warm and furry dog, by any chance?"

So it didn't work. He should have known it wouldn't. Using psychology on Jeffrey Stanley usually didn't. But because he really believed it was true and not just a pitch to get something he wanted, David gave it one more try.

"Well, it's just that what people dream about is usually very important, I mean if you want to understand about their problems and stuff like that."

"Look, son," Dad said. "I thought we'd had this out. No more pets for the time being. Okay? Now let's not discuss it any further."

"Okay." David shrugged and went back to washing the dishes. There wasn't any point in saying anything else. Even if he wasn't happy.

As soon as Dad and Molly were gone Amanda stuck her nose in the air. "Now let's not discuss it any further," she said in an uptight tone of voice that was supposed to be an imitation of Dad.

"Look," David said, "he only said that because Molly was listening. Before, when I asked him about getting a puppy, we discussed it a lot. What he said was, Molly would have to train it while we're all away at school, and she already doesn't have enough time to paint. That's why he wouldn't discuss it, so it wouldn't sound like he was blaming it on her."

"Yeah, well I still think it's pretty crummy," Amanda said. "You'd think that living way out here in the country where there's nothing to do, we could at least have a few animals around."

"I know," David said. "That's what I said, too. But Dad said we already did have a few animals, like Rolor and King Tut and Rocky."

"Animals," Amanda said. "Rolor and King Tut aren't animals. And Rocky isn't even ours."

It was true. Rolor was Blair's pet crow, and King Tut was a turkey. And Rocky was the beat up old tomcat who lived in the barn now and then when he wasn't off wandering around the country, looking for lady cats and getting into fights. And even when he was around, he wasn't all that friendly. In fact, nobody could even get near him, except Blair.

"Not that I care for myself," Amanda said. "I'm not all that crazy about dogs. But I don't see why you little kids can't have one."

Thanks a lot, Amanda, David thought. She knew how he felt about being classed with Janie and the twins as a little kid. The twins were barely six years old, and Janie was only eight. Thirteen was practically a whole different generation. But he'd learned from experience that having an argument with Amanda while she was supposed to be helping you clean up the kitchen was definitely what Dad called counterproductive. So he kept his mouth shut and only thought up a couple of very sarcastic remarks that he might have made if he'd been in the mood for an argument—or a crack over the head with a pancake turner, which was what he'd gotten the last time.

Fighting with Amanda under any circumstances had always been counterproductive, and lately it had become even more so. She'd always had the advantage of being a girl and therefore more or less unpunchable, even when she punched first. But in the last few months she'd acquired another unfair advantage by suddenly going from about David's height to at least six inches taller.

In the end he was more angry at himself for not telling her off, than he was at Amanda. It wasn't that he was a coward; at least, he didn't think it was. It was just that when it came right down to it, he never seemed able to get in the right frame of mind for a fight. And not being able to get in a fighting frame of mind was a real handicap when you were thirteen years old and in the eighth grade at Wilson Junior High.

Not, of course, that it hadn't been a problem before. David had known he wasn't particularly fond of fighting since he was a little kid, but he hadn't worried all that much about it. But then, he'd come back to the Steven's Corners school system after being away in Italy on his dad's sabbatical, had gone into eighth grade—and had met the Garvey Gang.

It had started off on the very first day of school, and of course he'd handled it all wrong. If he'd just gotten up and taken a swing at Garvey on that first day at the bus stop when Garvey had tripped him—no matter what happened afterwards . . .

"Hey, what's the matter with you?" Amanda practically yelled in his ear. Apparently she'd been yakking away for several minutes before she noticed that David wasn't doing much answering. She probably didn't even realize that her crack about little kids had bugged him. It figured.

"Nothing's the matter with me," he said, "except for dishpan hands. Look at them. Next time I'm going to dry."

Amanda was starting to argue, when all of a sudden she stopped and said, "Hey look. What's The Bleep doing?" Amanda thought it was funny to call Blair "The Bleep," because he sometimes talked so quietly you couldn't hear anything at all, like a bleeped out comment on TV.

David finished rinsing the sink and turned around in time to see Blair coming out of the pantry. He wasn't tiptoeing or anything, but he'd somehow managed to walk right past them into the pantry and then come out again, before they'd even noticed. And now he was just walking along smiling to himself and holding four slices of bread in front of him, two in each hand. When Esther got caught snitching food she always started stuffing it in her mouth so as to get as much eaten as possible before you could take it away. And if it had been Janie, she'd have had it carefully hidden so the only thing that tipped you off was the hammy wide-eyed-innocent number she always did when she was up to no good.

Nobody but Blair would walk along flatfooted, holding what he'd snitched right out in front of him. David grinned at Amanda, and she rolled her eyes and grinned back.

"Hey Blair," David said. "What're you doing with all that bread?"

"Bread?" Blair looked carefully at the two slices in his right hand, then the ones in his left. Then he looked at David and Amanda and nodded with a serious kind of smile and said, "He's very big."

"Who's big?" Amanda said. "What are you talking about? What's he talking about, David?"

"Blair," David said. "What are you talking about?"

"That dog," Blair said. "That big dog."

Chapter Two

"Was it gone, Blair? Did he come and eat it?"

"Yes, it's all gone."

What Esther and Blair were saying filtered into and mixed with a conversation between Owl and Pussy Gato that David was in the midst of reading. He was sprawled out on the couch peacefully enjoying the Sunday funnies—*Gordo* was his favorite strip—when the twins came into the room whispering. Yelling, he probably could have ignored—you got used to yelling kids in the Stanley family—but something about whispering makes it hard not to listen. So he tuned in on the twins and gave up, for the time being, on Pussy Gato.

He'd gotten up early that morning, not only to make Sunday last as long as possible, but also to have some time to be by himself. With five kids in the family it wasn't easy to find time alone, and once in a while he felt the need for a little solitude. So that morning he'd dressed very quietly and then tiptoed downstairs, trying to keep the ancient floor boards from squeaking.

He liked the feeling of being alone in the old house, listening to the silence and imagining that it was full of the unheard voices of all the people who had ever lived there. At least he liked it in the soft new brilliance of early morning. He knew from past experience that all alone in the Westerly House in the dark of night could be almost too interesting. But in the kitchen, early in the morning, the new day was already in high gear. The sun spilled in across the old-fashioned sink and sent a pathway of gold dust over the round oak table. David fixed himself a bowl of cereal and went out on the back steps to eat.

He ate slowly and peacefully, staring off across the backyard, past the old oak tree with its tire swing to where the land sloped down to the creek, and hearing nothing but birds and an occasional gobble from the direction of King Tut's pen. And then, when he'd finished eating, he strolled down the driveway, thinking about how the warm sunshine mixing with the cool autumn tingle in the air was something like the way the sour of lemons and the sweetness of sugar mixed to make the good taste of lemonade. At the mailbox, he picked up the Sunday paper and wandered back across the front yard, through the garden on the south side of the house with its gazebo and sundial, and back through the kitchen to the living room—where he'd been reading for quite a long time when Esther and Blair came in.

"Did you see him?" Esther whispered, and David moved the paper to one side and peeked around it. Esther was leaning toward Blair so that their heads were close together, Esther's sleek and brown and Blair's blond and curly. Esther's face was a pattern of circles—round cheeks, round eyes and mouth rounded into an "O" of excitement.

"No," Blair said. "Not today. Last night I did."

"See what?" David asked.

Esther looked around quickly, startled, but when she saw it was David she ran to him, pulling Blair after her.

"Blair's dog," she said. "Blair's dog was there again last night, and this morning the food we gave him was all gone."

"What food?" David asked.

"Oh, some bread," Esther said, rolling her eyes at Blair, "and some other things."

The morning before when David and Amanda had caught Blair coming out of the pantry, David had suggested that Blair put back all except one slice. "Why'd you let him keep that?" Amanda had asked. "Why can't an imaginary dog eat imaginary bread? It'll just go to waste." But apparently it hadn't exactly gone to waste. Something had eaten not only the slice of bread but "some other things" as well.

"Where was the food?" David asked Blair.

"In a pan," Esther said, answering for her twin, as usual. "In an old pan on the bench by the swing tree."

"And this morning it was gone?"

Blair nodded, and Esther said, "Yes. Yes, it was all gone this morning."

"Hmmm," David said. "Well, I guess a dog could have taken it, but there are other things around at night. Like raccoons and skunks and field mice."

"No," Esther said. "It was the dog. Because Blair saw

16

him. He couldn't see where the food was from the window, but the dog came and sat by the sundial like he always does. And he said thank you. Blair said he said thank you."

"Tesser," David said, reprovingly. Since she'd started school Esther had decided she didn't like to be called Tesser anymore, but it was a hard habit to break. Particularly when she was acting especially childish. She'd always gone along with Blair's wild stories, and a lot of the time she really seemed to believe them, but it didn't seem possible that she really could believe this one. And besides, Dad said that they should stop encouraging Blair's fantasies now that he was six years old and in school and everything. "Tesser, what are you talking about? Have you seen this dog of Blair's?"

"No." She shook her head thoughtfully. "But Blair's told me all about him. And Blair says I could see him. Blair says he's the kind of dog that I could see, too."

"Oh, yeah. Well, that's nice. Dogs you can see are definitely the best kind. Much better than invisible ones."

"Blair doesn't see invisible things," Esther said. "When something's invisible, nobody can see it, not even Blair. Blair just sees things that are different."

"Yeah," David said. "I know." He knew what Esther was referring to anyway. For a long time Esther and Janie had had this idea about Blair being able to see and hear things that other people couldn't. And there had been times in the past when David, himself, hadn't been too sure it wasn't true. But it was the kind of idea that most people grew out of somewhere along the line. David had grown out of it. At least most of the time he was pretty sure he had.

Just about then there was a clatter on the stairs and

Janie's voice yelling, "Twins! Twins! Where are you?" and a moment later she dashed into the room. "Oh, there you are," she said. "Why didn't you say so?"

"We were talking to David," Esther said, and then she clamped her mouth shut in a way that said, "and not anybody else."

Janie looked hard at Esther, and her big round blue eyes narrowed. She stared first at Blair and then at David. Then she squeezed in between the twins and put her arm across Esther's shoulders. She looked as if she'd just switched on to high beam, the way she always did when she was excited or curious. Dad always said that Janie had antennas for picking up other people's secrets, and right at the moment you could almost see them quivering on top of her head. "What are we talking about?" she said.

"My dog," Blair said, just as Esther stuck her face in front of his and shushed at him. Blair stared at her in surprise.

"You said it was a secret," she whispered at him. "You said you wouldn't tell anybody but me."

Blair looked worried. "No," he said. "You said I wouldn't. And you told David."

Esther put her hands on her waist. "Well, telling David doesn't count," she said, "because David already knew."

All the time Blair and Esther were arguing, Janie was saying, "What dog? What dog? Who's got a dog? Where is it?" And finally she yelled, "Shut up, Tesser! Shut up!"

"Shut up, yourself," Esther said. "It's Blair's dog, and it comes every night and sits out by the sundial. And it's very, very big."

Janie looked at David. "Really?" she asked. "Is there really a dog?"

David shrugged. "I don't know," he said. "I haven't seen it. Maybe there's a dog, but I think it might be a dream."

"No," Blair said. "It's not a dream dog."

"It's as tall as this," Esther went on, holding up her hand about as high as the top of her head, "and it has long legs and its face is all whiskery and it has great big eyes and sometimes they're red."

"Wowee," Janie said. "If I dreamed a dog like that, it'd be a nightmare. I think it's a nightmare, Blair."

Just about then Molly came in and said that breakfast was ready. So the dog conversation was over. After breakfast David got involved in working on the tree house Dad had helped him design for the little kids, and he forgot all about Blair's dream, or nightmare, until he was reminded that night, just as he was climbing into bed.

Blair was already asleep, and David was just getting propped up against the pillows for a little bedtime reading. He'd had to get up once because he'd forgotten to cover Rolor's cage, but now he was back in bed, and the only sound was an occasional cozy mumble from the crow as he settled himself for the night. David sighed comfortably and began to read just as the door opened and Esther and Janie came tiptoeing in.

"Hey," David said, "what's going on? You guys are supposed to be asleep."

"We came to see the dog," Janie said. "Come on, Tesser." They ran across the room, climbed up on the window seat and pressed their faces against the glass. When Janie cupped her hands around her eyes to shut out the light from the room, Esther did the same thing, and they went on kneeling there with their faces close together against the window and their bare feet and flowery pajama-bottoms sticking out over the edge of the window seat. David grinned. Several minutes passed in absolute silence. He sighed and went back to his book. Quite a long time later Janie said, "Do you see anything, Tesser?"

"I see the sundial," Esther said. "That's where he sits. Right there by the sundial. But I don't think he's there now."

And Janie said, "I don't think so either, but I'm not sure. I think we'd better get Blair."

"Okay," Esther said, "let's get him." They got down and ran to Blair's bed.

"Good luck," David said. He didn't bother to tell them not to wake Blair up because he was so sure they couldn't, but he hadn't counted on Janie's good ideas and Esther's stubbornness. They tried the usual things like shaking and tickling and bouncing, but when those didn't work, they tugged him to a sitting position, and then Esther propped him up while Janie pushed his eyelids open and made horrible faces at him. In a few minutes they had him sitting almost straight up on the window seat.

"Look, Blair," they said. "Is he there? Is the dog there yet?"

Blair swayed toward the window until his head was resting against the glass and stayed there—until Janie whacked him on top of the head. Then he jumped and said, "No. He's not there yet. Not yet." And then he curled up in a ball and went to sleep on the window seat.

David went back to reading, and after a while Esther and Janie gave up and started back to bed—leaving Blair where he was.

"Hey," David said. "You come right back here and put Blair back to bed."

Janie stopped in the doorway. She looked at Blair all curled up on the window seat and gave David one of her super-sweet smiles. "You're a lot stronger than we are," she said. "You could carry him."

"Huh-uh," David said. "You got him out—you can put him right back where you got him. I'm reading."

It was only fair, but afterwards David wished he'd just given up and done it himself. It took Janie and Esther so long to wake Blair up enough to walk him across the room that when it was finally over it was too late to do much reading. He'd only managed to read a few paragraphs, but with a seven thirty bus to catch the next morning, he knew he'd better stop.

It was a lot later when he woke up suddenly and sat up in bed. He'd been dreaming but he couldn't remember what, except that he'd been running, trying to get away from something, and all of a sudden a dog was running beside him. The dog looked up at him and barked, and suddenly David was awake and sitting up, and feeling that something wasn't right. Across the room, Blair's bed was dissolved in darkness but somehow, even before his groping fingers found the lamp switch, he knew that Blair wasn't there. He wasn't in his bed, or standing by the window, or anywhere else in the room.

David went first to the window, and just as he reached it, before his eyes had finished adjusting to the change in light, he thought he saw something in the yard below. It looked like a beam of light, and it seemed to come from a spot near the gate that led from the garden into the backyard. But then it was gone, and in the dark window David could see only the reflection of the room behind him. Running to his lamp, he switched it off and hurried back to the window.

Gradually, as his eyes became accustomed to the darkness, he began to recognize the dimly seen shapes in the garden below. The moon wasn't very full, but there was enough light to see the white gazebo quite clearly. Next to it the gray stone of the sundial's pedestal was barely visible, and just beyond that the big pine tree near the gate threw its long dark shadow across the lawn. But surely he'd be able to see a big dog, even if it were in the shadow. He'd have been able to see it, that is, if it had been there. But, of course, it wasn't. No dog, and no six-year-old kid in blue pajamas, either. But Blair had to be somewhere, and somebody had to find out where. As Molly said, sleepwalkers sometimes fell down stairs, or out of windows.

About one minute later when David was on his way downstairs, he met Blair coming up. He was wearing slippers and carrying David's flashlight, and if he was sleepwalking, he must have been dreaming that he was wide awake. Before, when he'd found Blair sleepwalking, David had been careful not to speak to him, but this time he decided to take the chance.

"Blair?" he said.

"Hi, David," Blair said.

David took the flashlight out of Blair's hand and shone it on his face. Blair blinked and smiled. When you shine a flashlight right on someone's face, it makes most people look weird and evil, but not Blair. On Blair it just turned his hair into a curly halo and made his Christmas-card-angel face look even more so. "Hi," he said again in the eager, breathless way he always talked when he was excited. David sighed. He knew what the answer was going to be before he asked the question.

Chapter
Three

It took David quite a while to get back to sleep. A long time after Blair's breathing had shifted to a deep steady rhythm and he'd started making occasional little murmuring noises, David lay stiffly on his back trying to keep his mind a blank. A blank mind, he knew from experience, was the best kind at that hour of the night. In the evening when he'd just gone to bed, he never tried to keep his mind from free-wheeling. At that time of night he could dream up whatever he wanted to and make it all turn out great, like a video game that he was so good at he could win every time. But late at night, when he'd been asleep and then awake again, it all got out of control. As if the joy stick was disconnected and all the bombs were hitting you dead center and the blue meanies were gobbling up your Pac-Man. And Pete Garvey was punching you out in front of the whole school, and

Blair's dog was real and dangerous, or even some kind of a werewolf.

That night most of the gruesome scenes that kept appearing in front of his closed eyelids had to do with what Blair had told him. When David met him coming back up the stairs, Blair had been very excited. Excited and wide awake. David would almost swear to that. As a matter of fact, David couldn't remember ever having heard Blair talk so much and so fast, and it didn't seem likely a person could talk better asleep than awake. One of the first things Blair said was that the dog had licked him on the cheek.

"He licked me right here," he'd told David, pointing to his cheek. "And he let me pat him." Blair's teeth were chattering and his hands were cold as ice. "I p-p-p-patted him," he said. "He never let me pat him before."

David got him into bed and tucked him in, but he kept popping back up again. His cheeks were so red they looked painted, and his eyes glittered with excitement. He told David all about the dog—how it was taller than his head and how its fur was long and gray, and how big and white its teeth were when it smiled at him.

"Smiled at you?" David asked.

"Like this." Blair lifted his lip in what looked like an exaggerated smile—or what, on another kind of face, might have been a growl. David felt a shiver run up the back of his neck like a cold finger.

"Okay," he said. "But don't go out there at night anymore. Okay?"

"But that's when he's there," Blair said. "He's not there when it's daytime."

"I don't care," David said. "You shouldn't ever go outside at night, all alone like that."

"I wasn't alone," Blair said. "That dog was there."

The conversation started going in circles after that and then Blair went to sleep—and David lay awake trying, without much success, to keep his mind a blank. The problem was that at that time of night he found himself taking seriously a lot of ideas that he would probably have laughed at in the daylight. Ideas like ghosts dogs, or werewolves. There wasn't any such thing, of course, but if there were, a kid like Blair might see them when other people couldn't. A kid who just possibly saw and talked to a ghost named Harriette, who was a real person who once lived in the Westerly House and who some people thought still lived there, even though she was dead. And a kid who seemed able to talk to all sorts of animals, like crows and turkeys—not to mention wild cats that nobody else could get close to.

Those were the kinds of ideas that kept pushing into David's mind, sometimes in words and sometimes in vivid pictures that turned the inside of his eyelids into wide-screen horror movies. Pictures of a dark garden where a very small boy stood alone and helpless while something moved closer and closer through the shadows—something huge and shaggy with gleaming red eyes and huge white fangs in a gaping mouth. At some point the waking horror movies turned into sleeping ones, and when he woke up the next morning David could remember a lot of bits and pieces of scary dog dreams. Blair's nightmare seemed to be catching.

Dad and Molly overslept that morning, and everything

was very rushed and hectic. There wasn't time to tell Dad about the latest development in the dog story, and by that evening David had decided not to tell. He couldn't very well admit that he'd stayed awake for hours worrying about Blair playing with a werewolf. And it was pretty obvious how Dad would take it if he only told him—again—that Blair had been dreaming about a dog. It was, David decided, a lot like the story of the boy who cried wolf, or dog, as the case might be.

"Now, let's not discuss it any further." David could just hear it. So he wouldn't discuss it, and he definitely wouldn't worry about it. As it happened it was a resolution that was fairly easy to keep, because the next day turned out to be a different kind of nightmare. Afterwards, there was something new to worry about.

In a way, Mrs. Baldwin, David's homeroom teacher, was to blame. What she did was to get called away to some sort of emergency meeting. When the messenger from the office brought the note, Mrs. Baldwin read it and said, "Oh drat!" and started looking around the room while she got out her purse and put on her sweater. Almost immediately, even before he had consciously figured out what she was up to, David started having a kind of premonition—a feeling that something terrible was about to happen. Premonitions ran in the family on his mother's side. His mother had had them, and of course Blair did. Blair's premonitions usually came true, and David's usually didn't. Except for certain kinds. Like now, when he seemed to be getting a warning that fate, or something, was about to pull the rug out from under him.

He was trying to lie low, squnching down and pretending to look for something in his desk, to get out of Mrs. Baldwin's range of vision, when she called his name.

"David," he heard her say, "David Stanley. Would you come up here, please."

"Me?" he said, warily. By then he had guessed what was about to happen. It wasn't the first time. For some reason it had been going on all his life. Teachers who had to leave the room picked him out to be in charge while they were gone. He had never wanted to be. Even in the first or second grade when nearly everyone raised a hand if the teacher asked for a volunteer, he had not wanted to be in charge of the class. And now, in the eighth grade—in the eighth grade at Wilson Junior High with Maribell Montgomery and Holly Rayburn giggling and the Garvey Gang raising their eyebrows at each other—there was nothing in the world he wanted less.

"I'd rather not . . ." he started to say, but Mrs. Baldwin ignored him and started telling the class what they should be working on while she was gone. Then she was standing beside David's desk and picking up his books. "Just bring your things up to my desk, David. All you'll have to do is keep an eye on things and jot down the name of anyone who starts wasting the taxpayers' money." Mrs. Baldwin always called any kind of fooling around "wasting the taxpayers' money."

He tried once more to protest, but she didn't seem to hear him. A few seconds later she was gone, and David was sitting in her chair in front of everybody. He huddled down as low as he could get, wishing he could disappear and thinking up all the things he should have said to Mrs. Baldwin.

"Look," he should have said, "this is ridiculous. Someone's in charge of this class, all right, when no teachers are around, but it isn't me. It is definitely, absolutely, positively not David Stanley. Look at me, Mrs. Baldwin. Do I look like the in-charge type?"

Over the top of the book he was hiding behind, David stole a glance at the five rows of eighth graders. What Mrs. Baldwin didn't seem to have noticed was that people in the eighth grade tend to come in a great variety of sizes, and most of them were a lot bigger than David Stanley.

At one time, only a couple of years ago, in fact, David had been of about average classroom size, but that was no longer true. He didn't think he was actually shrinking, but it was obvious that he hadn't been doing nearly enough growing. Nearly everyone was bigger than he was now, even the girls. Particularly the girls. There were, as a matter of fact, about ten people in the room who were about a foot taller than he was, and nine of them were girls. The other one was Pete Garvey. Pete Garvey was fourteen, almost six feet tall, and at the moment he was talking in a loud voice.

He started out by asking his friends questions about the assignment, and then he began to make comments about Holly's new sweater. Everyone laughed about the comments, and Pete got louder.

David couldn't decide what to do. At first he kept his head down and his eyes on his book, pretending he hadn't noticed. His face was hot and his teeth were clamped together so tightly his jaws ached. It wasn't any of his business what Garvey did, and Mrs. Baldwin had no right to try to make it his business. But the laughter kept getting louder, and David finally realized how funny he must look pretending not to notice. So he started laughing, too. Or, at least trying to.

"That sweater sure looks good from back here," Garvey said. After a second or two he stood up and said, "Think I'll just check to see if Holly needs any help with the assignment. You need any help, Holly? I'm real good at this metric stuff."

The class cracked up. Pete was very good at some things, but none of them had anything to do with schoolwork. If Pete had been good at schoolwork, he obviously would have been in the ninth grade at least. Grinning at David, he got out of his seat, sauntered up the aisle to Holly's seat, and leaned over it. Holly ducked and giggled, and the whole class laughed—and watched David to see what he was going to do. Pete looked around the room, and then he swaggered on up to Mrs. Baldwin's desk. He leaned on the desk staring at David.

"Hey, Stanley," he said. "You put down my name like the teacher said?"

David stopped pretending to laugh. "Not me," he said. "I didn't ask to . . ."

But Garvey drowned him out. "Hey, lookee here," he said. "Old Stanley didn't jot me down like the teacher told him. I'm real shocked, Stanley. A good kid like you, not doing what the teacher says." He stared at David, and David forced himself to stare back.

"I told you . . ." he was trying to say, but Garvey went on.

"You know what I think? I think a good kid like you would of put me down if he wasn't afraid. You afraid to write me down, Stanley?"

Suddenly it was very quiet. David's whole face seemed to

be throbbing. "No," he heard himself saying. "I'm not afraid." He picked up his pen and tried to keep his hand from shaking as he wrote Garvey's name on Mrs. Baldwin's tablet.

"Hey, hey," Garvey was saying, "look what Davy's doing," when the door opened and Mrs. Baldwin walked in.

The nightmare was over—for the time being. Garvey tried to argue, but Mrs. Baldwin wouldn't listen to him. She buzzed the principal's office and said she was sending Pete Garvey over immediately. Then she took Garvey's arm and led him out of the room. He went quietly. When Mrs. Baldwin put people out of her room, they went quietly—even Pete Garvey. Mr. Prentice, the principal, was very rough on people who got sent to the office. Garvey was, obviously, going to be in a lot of hot water. But, even more obviously, so was David. He knew it even before one of Garvey's friends, Ace Maillard, cornered him and told him so.

Mrs. Baldwin's class ended at ten o'clock in the morning, so when it was finished, there were still about five and a half hours until time to catch the bus for home. It seemed more like five and a half centuries. David's head was so full of what had happened, and what was going to happen, that what was actually happening couldn't seem to get through to him. He got yelled at in P.E. for not being on his toes in the outfield and called down in English for having to say, "What was the question?" when Mr. Edmonds called on him. Toward the end of the day, he spent most of the time thinking about what was going to happen at the bus stop.

All the bus riders from the high school as well as the junior high waited in the parking lot. The buses were usually late coming back from taking the little kids home, and all kinds of things went on during the waiting. Classes were over for the day, and everybody was in the mood to let off steam. Amanda said waiting for the bus was the best part of her day, and there had been times when David felt the same way. He was pretty sure today wasn't going to be one of them.

Last period was almost over when he finally had a good idea. He would visit Mrs. Parker. Mrs. Parker had been his sixth grade, and all-time favorite, teacher, and he hadn't been over to visit her for a long time. The elementary school was just across the parking lot from the junior high, and you could see the bus stop area from the windows of her room.

There was still the locker problem. Right after the dismissal bell rang, he usually went to his locker, and that was probably where Garvey would look for him first. So he wouldn't be there. Asking the teacher for a pass to the restroom, he stopped off at his locker and got out everything he needed to take home—so, when the final bell rang, he'd be able to go in the opposite direction. Out the north door, around behind the building, and across the parking lot—and fast.

It worked. No one had arrived at the bus stop when David hurried across the far end of the parking lot. Mrs. Parker was glad to see him. She was feeding the animals—Mrs. Parker was famous for her menageries—and David offered to help. While they chatted about old times, he cleaned out the guinea pigs' cage and fed the tropical fish—and kept an eye on the parking lot. Pete Garvey was there, all right, clowning around as usual—barging in and out of groups and slapping people on the back.

"It's really nice to see you again," Mrs. Parker said while David was doing a extra thorough job of cleaning out the baby chickens' pen, "but I don't want to make you miss the bus. Isn't it about due?"

On his way to the sink to scrub out the water dish, David looked out the window. "The bus isn't there yet. I've got plenty of time," he was saying, when suddenly there it was, pulling into the lot. He filled the dish and ran back to the cage, sloshing water, and then dashed out the door, yelling a few final remarks on the way. Garvey was already on the bus, and the driver was Mr. Hobbs, who didn't stand for any fooling around, so everything was all right—for the moment.

Amanda had been busy flirting when David scrambled on the bus, just as Mr. Hobbs was reaching for the door handle. He didn't think she'd even noticed him arriving late. But that night, while they were doing their homework, he discovered that she had.

They were working at the dining room table. In the evening the dining room was a Quiet Zone—reserved for homework. As usual, Dad was there too, reading the newspaper, in order to get away from the TV, which was in the living room.

"Hey," Amanda leaned forward and whispered. "Did you have to stay after school today, or what? You almost missed the bus."

David had almost figured out what formula to use to solve the algebra problem he was working on. He tried to keep what he had almost remembered in mind as he answered. "No. I just went over to visit Mrs. Parker, and she asked me to clean out some cages."

"Oh yeah. Well, someone was looking for you."

The formula disappeared. "Who?" he asked, knowing what the answer would be.

"Pete Garvey. He said he wanted to tell you something. He asked me where you were. He said he had something he wanted to tell his old buddy, David." Amanda looked curious. "I didn't know you were friends with Pete Garvey."

David's grin was sarcastic, but Amanda didn't seem to notice. "Neither did I," he said.

"Why don't you ask him over sometime," Amanda said.

There was something about the sound of her voice that clued him in. He stared at her. Sure enough. She had that glazed look in her eyes that she always got when she was starting to flip out. Ever since the seventh grade when Amanda's favorite hobby switched from the supernatural to the opposite sex, she'd been flipping out over a new guy about every other week.

"Don't tell me you're interested in an eighth grader," he said. "An eighth grader with the brains of a kindergartener."

Amanda grinned. "I don't care what grade his brains are in. What Eloise and I like are his muscles. We think he's a real hunk."

"Ye gods," David said.

Chapter
Four

For the next day or two David spent a great deal of time and energy on planning. Like a general mapping out the movements of an army, he plotted and charted, arranging advances and retreats according to where Pete Garvey wasn't likely to be at any particular moment. It was, he thought, a lot like the riddle about the man with a small boat and a fox, a goose and a bag of corn. The goose-David had to be separated from the fox-Garvey, except when a boatman-teacher was present.

He made sure to arrive at math and art, the only classes he shared with Garvey, very early or very late. Between classes he moved quickly and alertly, and by unusual routes. But catching the bus for home continued to be the biggest problem. On the second afternoon he went again to visit Mrs. Parker. This time the cages were still pretty clean, and Mrs.

Parker was busy helping a sixth grader named Scooter with his long division.

"Well, David," she said, looking surprised. "Back so soon. How nice," and then, "No, Scooter, subtract. The next step is subtract, isn't it?" Scooter grinned at David, obviously grateful for the interruption. Mrs. Parker tapped sharply on the desk.

"Subtract?" the kid said, and bent over his paper, but his eyes kept slipping sideways to steal curious glances at David.

"I—er—I," David stammered, and then, "I didn't leave a library book here, did I? I mean, I think I had this library book with me when—"

"I don't believe so," Mrs. Parker said. "I didn't notice it. What was the title?"

"The title? Oh, you mean—the title. I don't exactly remember the title but it was about—dogs. It was a book about dogs."

Mrs. Parker looked at him strangely. He had a strong feeling that she knew he was lying, but she didn't say so. Instead she invited him to look around for his book.

For a few minutes he poked around among the animal cages pretending to search, but the kid kept staring at him, and Mrs. Parker kept having to say, "Scooter. Pay attention." So he didn't stay very long.

Out in the hall, he spent some time examining the works of art on the bulletin boards. The ones near the door to the parking lot were self-portraits by kindergarteners. Two teachers, a parent, and five or six kids walked by while David stood around pretending to be fascinated by a lot of round heads with u-shaped smiles and arms coming out of their ears. He felt ridiculous. It wasn't worth it, he decided. He was going to stop hiding and dodging and get it over with. After all, it wouldn't actually kill him if Garvey did beat him up. At least, he didn't think it would. He took a deep breath, squared his shoulders and marched out the door—just as the bus was turning into the parking lot.

Garvey was there all right, playfully twisting one of his friend's arms. The friend, a skinny guy named Jerry, was yelling and pleading. Garvey looked right at David, but he was having such a good time breaking his friend's arm that he didn't stop in time, and David got safely onto the bus.

That night David had a terrible dream about being chased all over Steven's Corners by Pete Garvey. The dream woke him up, and while he was lying awake thinking about it, he changed his mind about getting it over with. If that meant a couple of black eyes and a split lip, it seemed worthwhile to try all other possibilities first. Maybe, if he could stay out of Garvey's way long enough for somebody else to do something Garvey didn't like, that person would take over the top spot on his hit list. In the meantime, David decided, he would solve the bus problem by riding his bike to school. It was a long ride, but if he got up extra early and rode very fast, he thought he could make it.

It wasn't easy. He arrived at school tired and sweaty, and in the afternoon he got home very late. Worst of all, the second day it rained. There had only been a few clouds in the sky that morning, but by afternoon there were a lot more. A few minutes after David started for home it began to drizzle.

By the time he got home, he was soaked and freezing and very tired. As he turned down the driveway of the Westerly House, the rain started coming down in torrents.

Inside the garage, a tall, squarish building that had once been a stable, he climbed stiffly off his bike and shook himself like a wet dog. Water sprayed all around him. As he crossed the floor, pushing the bike, he left a wide wet trail, like some kind of giant snail. He was looking around for something to dry his hands on before he got his books out of the bike bag, when he heard voices.

He stood very still listening. Overhead the rain roared on the wooden shingles, but mingling with the rain sound was the steady rise and fall of a human voice. For just a moment he wondered if he were cracking up, or if . . . The back of his neck began to tingle as he thought of Blair's mysterious friend Harriette, who supposedly was still hanging around the premises from time to time. The tingle got stronger and began to creep down his spine.

He was just about to dump his bicycle and get out of there when the rain let up a little, and in the comparative quiet, the voice came through more clearly. It was Janie's. Only Janie yakking away in the hayloft, directly over his head. He tiptoed toward the ladder.

When his head and shoulders were above the level of the loft floor, David stopped. Janie, Blair and Esther were sitting in the middle of the loft on a pile of old gunny sacks. Janie was facing away from the ladder, and the twins were so wrapped up in what she was saying that they didn't notice David either. He stood very still and listened.

"No, they wouldn't." Janie was shaking her head.

"They'd never let us. Remember those guinea pigs Jennifer was going to give me? We're just going to have to keep him an absolute secret. Absolute, Tesser. And you're going to have to stop talking about him, Blair."

"Can't we even tell David?" Esther said.

"I don't know." Janie paused for a minute and then shook her head slowly. "I don't think we'd better. He's a very bad liar."

"Who's a bad liar?" Esther said.

"David is," Janie said.

"David is not a bad liar," Esther said.

"Hi, David," Blair said.

Janie and Esther whirled around, big-eyed and guilty-looking.

"Well, well," David said. "What's the big secret? And who says I'm a bad liar?"

Janie jumped to her feet.

"Hi, David," Esther said. "We were just talking about Blair's—ouch! You stepped on me. That hurt, Janie." She jumped up and gave Janie a push, and Janie shoved her back. They were still pushing each other and yelling when Dad's car drove into the garage and, of course, he heard the yelling and made them all come down out of the loft and explain themselves.

Janie and Esther were both trying to explain without telling him anything when, luckily, Dad noticed how wet David was. By the time he got through with his lecture on how chills could lead to colds and flu and pneumonia, he'd forgotten about the yelling. And David had forgotten all about what he'd overheard in the loft. At least for the time being. He remembered, though, a little later that night, when Dad started in about Mrs. Bowen's letter.

David was in the dining room nodding out over his homework—the bicycle routine was really getting to him—when Dad came in and asked him to come into the living room for a few minutes for a family conference. About Blair, he said.

"About Blair? What's the matter with Blair?"

Dad smiled. "Nothing new. Come on. It'll be faster to tell everyone at the same time."

The whole family was in the living room, except for Blair, who apparently had conked out a few minutes before and been carried up to bed, as usual. Blair had always needed a lot of sleep, but lately he seemed to be falling asleep even earlier than usual. Janie and Esther were watching TV, Amanda was curled up in her favorite chair, and Molly was standing by the fireplace looking worried. As soon as he had turned off the TV and asked everyone for their attention, Dad sat down and took an envelope out of his jacket pocket. He looked at it for a minute before he started in about how he'd just gotten the letter from Blair's teacher.

"Mrs. Bowen is very concerned about Blair," he said. "Apparently he's been sharing some of his fantasies with the class, and Mrs. Bowen feels he's too wrapped up in them. Out of touch with reality, she calls it. She sees it as a real problem. And she seems to think we can all help."

Molly sighed impatiently. "It's so ridiculous," she said.

Dad frowned. "I don't see it as ridiculous. I don't know that I agree with her assessment of the seriousness of the situation, but I do agree that we're all somewhat to blame. It seems to me we've all been guilty of encouraging Blair in his fantasies. Particularly you kids."

At that point David flashed on what he'd overheard in the garage. He couldn't remember exactly what the kids had been saying, but what he did recall was enough to make him realize how right Dad was. Janie and Esther had undoubtedly been encouraging Blair to think that his nightmare dog was the real thing.

"I know you all enjoy the great stories Blair makes up," Dad went on, "and I certainly don't blame you for that. There's no doubt that he has a very fertile imagination. But I think Mrs. Bowen may be right when she says that a person Blair's age should be better able to distinguish between fantasy and reality. And I think we can all help him to do just that."

"Okay," Janie said, "we'll help. I'm very good at distinguishing. Distinguishing is something that detectives are very good at."

"Me too," Esther said. "I want to help, too. How are you going to do it, Janie? How do we extinguish Blair?"

Dad smiled, and Molly laughed out loud. "I think you're absolutely right, Tesser honey," Molly said. "Extinguish is the right word. That woman wants to extinguish something that is uniquely and wonderfully Blair." Molly's face looked flushed, and there was something about the way she looked at Dad that made David feel a little uneasy.

Amanda was grinning. "What's The Bleep been telling those poor little old first graders? I'll bet he's been giving them a real thrill."

Molly smiled at Amanda. "He's been talking about Harriette, for one thing. Apparently," Molly said, "Blair told some of the children he has an invisible friend named Harriette who lives in our house."

"No," Esther said. "Blair doesn't say Harriette is invisible. He says we could see her if she came out when we were around—if we looked hard enough. He says we're usually just not looking hard enough."

"I see," Dad said. "Well, however that may be, Mrs. Bowen thinks it would be better for Blair if we would all help him to realize that Harriette is just a game. And the dog, too."

David happened to be looking at Janie, and when Dad mentioned the dog, her mouth flew open in a kind of gasp and snapped shut again. Then she looked hard at Esther and shook her head. Dad must have heard the gasp because he turned to look at her. "What did you say, Janie?" he asked.

"I just said, 'Tsk, tsk.' " Janie shook her head disapprovingly. "Tsk, tsk. That Blair! Telling all those kids at school about his imaginary dog!" Dad looked at Janie for a moment before he went on. It was pretty obvious to David that Janie was up to something, and he was sure Dad was thinking the same thing. But after a moment Dad went on about how they shouldn't accuse Blair of lying because Blair's fantasies were very real to him, but they should all let him know that they realized Harriette and the dog, and all the rest, were simply a kind of game.

Right in the middle of what Dad was saying, Molly sighed loudly, turned her back and stared into the fire. David looked quickly at Dad, but if he had noticed he was pretending he hadn't. Still David had that uncomfortable, tight feeling between his shoulder blades that he'd always gotten when somebody was trying to start a fight at school, particularly if they were trying to start it with him. Which was strange, because he'd always thought he felt that way because he was afraid. He certainly wasn't afraid when Dad and Molly got into an argument, he just didn't like it.

"Okay," Dad was saying in a kind of phony super-cheerful voice. "Everybody got it? Will you all promise to stop pretending to believe in Blair's fantasies?"

Esther looked worried. "Do we have to promise to stop believing in . . ." she was saying when Janie interrupted.

"We promise," she said loudly. "We promise not to pretend to believe in anything unless we really do believe in it, because then it wouldn't be pretending because it would be really, and when something's really you don't have to pretend. That's okay, isn't it? That's okay, Tesser. Can we go now?"

Dad grinned. "I'm afraid you lost me on that one. Just tell Blair to knock it off if he starts telling everyone about Harriette and the dog."

"We already did that," Esther said. "Didn't we, Janie? We already told Blair to stop telling . . . hey, turn loose, Janie. Where are we going?"

After Janie had dragged Esther out of the room, Molly stopped staring into the fire and went out too. David stayed where he was for a while watching. After Molly went out, Dad went on sitting in the same place, staring at the letter from Mrs. Bowen before he threw it down on the coffee table and kind of stalked out of the room.

"What's the matter with you?" Amanda said.

"Who me?" David asked.

"Yeah, you. You're twitching." Amanda screwed up her face and jerked her shoulders around.

"Oh that," David said. "I've got a stiff neck. Too much bicycle riding, I guess."

Chapter Five

The next day was Saturday, and David decided to go hiking. Ever since the Stanleys had moved into the Westerly House, he'd enjoyed hiking in the rolling hills that started just beyond the back yard. Sometimes he took the little kids with him, but he really preferred to go alone. Alone he could move at his own pace and quietly. Moving slowly and silently he'd been able to get very close to lots of squirrels and birds, and once he'd even been only a few yards from a doe with twin fawns. Hiking, he'd found, was a good way to take your mind off things you'd just as soon not think about, which right at the moment seemed like a particularly good idea.

Fortunately Janie and the twins had just left for an all day birthday party, so he wasn't expecting any trouble getting away by himself. He was in the kitchen fixing a lunch to take along when Amanda came in and leaned on the counter.

"What's that for?" she asked.

He grinned. "Well, actually, I was thinking of eating it."

"Very funny. I mean why are you putting it in your backpack?"

"Because I'm going hiking," he said, and then because he was sure she'd say no, he added, "You want to come along?"

Amanda grabbed a piece of cheese he'd just sliced off for his sandwich and stuck it in her mouth. "Sure," she said with her mouth full. "Why not?"

David stared at her. "I thought you hated hiking."

"I do. But right at the moment I'm having a totally fatal attack of boredom."

He stifled a sigh. He'd really been looking forward to getting away all by himself. However, he'd never been hiking with Amanda before, except for a couple of times in Italy when a lot of other people were along, too. Maybe it wouldn't be too bad. "Well," he said, "if it's either hiking or sudden death . . ."

Amanda grabbed the last slice of baloney and began to make a sandwich.

The first part of the hike went better than David had expected. On the long slope that led up to the hills, she walked quickly, and later, when the going got rough, she didn't get nervous about the steep places. And when David suggested they might see some animals if they were quiet, she stopped talking, at least for a while. It was a nice day, clean and clear after the rain, with a damp earthy smell under the trees and the winter grass beginning to show green on the hillsides. They saw two squirrels having a noisy argument and watched a big red-tailed hawk diving out of the sky to catch a field mouse or small gopher and carry it away to the top of a big oak tree. At the top of the first ridge, they found a shady spot under a bunch of bay trees and ate their lunch and talked.

Amanda said that so far the hike hadn't been as bad as she'd expected, and that watching the hawk had been gross but kind of exciting. Then David mentioned the squirrels, and Amanda said they'd reminded her of Eloise and Tammy. Eloise and Tammy were two girls in Amanda's class who were her best friends—except when there'd just been some kind of a fight and one or both of them totally grossed her out.

"Yeah," Amanda said. "That dark gray one with the fat cheeks was Tammy. She was telling Eloise that she used to feel sorry for her because she thought she was a victim of child abuse, until she realized that her black eyes were just too much eye shadow.

David laughed. "She didn't really say that to Eloise, did she?"

"Sure," Amanda said. "In a loud voice in the cafeteria line. And then Eloise—the one with the long skinny tail—said she was really surprised to hear that Tammy had been worrying about her because she'd always thought that fat people never worried about anything—except maybe what was for lunch."

"Wow," David said. "I thought they were real good friends."

"They are. They're crazy about each other."

"Then how come they . . ."

"That was last week. This week they're mad at me. They went to the Doom Flume today, and they both called me up to tell me I wasn't invited. That's why I didn't have anything to do."

David was curious. Amanda sounded slightly sarcastic, but not too upset. Maybe she was just hiding it. "Well, next week they'll probably hate each other and be crazy about you," he said.

Amanda shrugged. "I couldn't care less. They both totally gross me out."

David nodded. It figured. Personally he wasn't too good at insulting people, whether they happened to be his best friends or not. But with Amanda he guessed it kind of came naturally.

When they'd finished eating, David said that he'd planned to go over the next ridge and then on down into the valley to a little lake where animals sometimes came to drink—but they could go back now if Amanda was tired.

"Who's tired?" Amanda said. "I'm beginning to like this 'Wild Kingdom' stuff."

So they went on, and when they were almost to the top of the next range of hills, they begin to hear the dirt bikes. Even before they got to where they could see anything, he could tell they were dirt bikes because of the noise they made.

"We might as well go back," he told Amanda. "There

won't be any animals in a hundred miles with all that noise going on."

"Come on," she said. "Let's see who it is. I know some guys who have dirt bikes."

So they went on climbing, and when they reached the crest of the hill the noise got a whole lot louder. Directly down below them, where some little rolling foothills surrounded the narrow valley, little clouds of exhaust were rising up into the sky, and in two or three places you could see where the bikes had torn away the grass in a network of deep muddy trails. As they watched, a bike came shooting into view, flew over the top of a rise and plunged down the other side.

"Hey. I know him," Amanda said. "He's in my history class. His name is Greg. Let's go on down. Maybe they'll give us a ride."

"Well," David said, "I don't know." He wasn't feeling too enthusiastic about the whole thing even before the second bike came over the top of the hill. But when it did, he stopped in his tracks. There was no way Amanda was going to talk him into going any farther. The guy riding the bike was Pete Garvey.

Amanda had already started out, but when she realized David was staying right where he was, she stopped. "Well, come on," she said.

"No way. Did you see who that was? On that last bike?"

"No. Who was it?"

"Pete Garvey."

"So? I thought he was a friend of yours."

"Look," David said. "I hate to disappoint you, but that

day Garvey told you he was looking for me, it wasn't because he's my friend. He was looking for me because he wanted to punch me out."

"Punch you out? Why would Garvey want to punch you out? He's twice as big as you are."

"Actually, I'd noticed that," David said sarcastically. "And I wouldn't be surprised if Garvey has, too. I think he prefers to punch out people who are smaller than he is."

Amanda looked at David with a funny expression. "Okay," she said. "He wants to punch you out. Why?"

So David sat down on a rock and started telling her the whole story. Before he'd gotten very far, she sat down too and listened very carefully. She seemed interested, but it was obvious that she didn't take it seriously because she kept grinning. David didn't think it was all that funny.

When David finished, Amanda said it reminded her of something that happened in the school she used to go to before Molly and Dad got married—some guy caller Killer Keller used to beat up on everyone. But right in the middle of a particularly gory part about what Killer did to some little guy who tried to fight back, she stopped suddenly and said, "Hey, listen."

"I don't hear anything."

"I know," she said. "That's what I meant. They're gone."

Sure enough, the roar of the dirt bikes was gone, and all you could hear was the usual soft natural sounds of the valley—the rustle of the wind and now and then the distant chirping of a bird. After a while Amanda suggested that they go on down to the lake. David wasn't too sure he wanted to. It was possible that the bikers were just taking a rest. So he asked Amanda to finish telling her story first. It was quite a long story with lots of gruesome details, and when she finally finished, there still was no sign of the dirt bikers. "See," Amanda said. "The coast is clear. Come on."

The first part of the trail down to the valley floor was fairly steep, but near the bottom it leveled out. Just before it turned toward the lake, there was a place where it forked. One of the branches led on down the slope toward the road that went over another rise and into Fillmore Valley. David was leading the way. He had just turned onto the valley trail, when he circled some bushes and practically ran into someone who was coming down the path in the other direction. It was Pete Garvey.

"Hey." Garvey grabbed David by the shoulder. "Lookee here."

David tried to pull away, but it was no use. Garvey was grinning, but the smile didn't make David feel any better.

"What're you doing out here?" Garvey said.

"We were hiking." Amanda had caught up. "What are you doing?"

Garvey looked at Amanda. "Hey," he said. "What'cha doing with this little twerp?"

"David felt Amanda bump against his shoulder, but he didn't dare take his eyes off Garvey to look at her. "He's my brother," Amanda said. "What are you going to do?"

"Well, now," Garvey said slowly. "I been looking for this little twerp for a long time." His grip tightened on David's shoulder, and he lifted his arm, pulling David up onto his tiptoes. "I got a bone to pick with this little twerp."

David wished he'd get it over with—and that he'd quit

51

saying "little twerp." He wished it so hard he was actually clenching his fist to take a desperate and useless swing at Garvey's grinning face, when all of a sudden a fist shot out of nowhere and smashed right into the middle of it. For a weird second or two he almost thought the fist might have been his own, but of course it wasn't.

Garvey turned loose of David and stepped back with both hands over his nose. It had been a very hard punch. David winced. He could almost feel it himself. He was still standing there staring at Garvey when Amanda grabbed him by the arm and almost jerked him off his feet. "Come on," she said. "Let's get out of here."

A few feet down the trail he turned around and looked back. Garvey had turned loose of his nose, but he was still just standing there, in exactly the same place he'd been when Amanda hit him, as if he were frozen to the spot. The expression on his face was even blanker than usual.

"David," Amanda said. "Are you coming—or what?" David hurried after her. He didn't look back again, but for quite a while he kept expecting to hear Garvey charging after them; but he never did. After a while he quit worrying about it. By the time they got to the ridge, he was worrying about something else. Amanda wasn't acting like herself.

At first he couldn't exactly put his finger on it. It was a little bit as if she were mad at him—but not exactly. Several times he caught her staring at him; but when he tried to talk to her, she answered briefly, as if she were angry or else had something on her mind and didn't want to be interrupted.

Once, just trying to make conversation, David said, "That must have really hurt."

"What?" Amanda said, and then she looked at her hand with a strange kind of surprised expression and said, "Yeah, it did. It hurt a lot."

"Oh," David said. He hadn't thought about her hand; but now that he did, he realized what she meant. He'd heard of people breaking the bones in their hands by punching other people. "I hope it's not broken or anything."

Amanda stopped and stared at him for a second. She looked irritated, as if there were something about him she really resented. "Forget it," she said.

He didn't try to talk anymore. He'd begun to figure it out. She'd probably just realized what a coward he was, and she was really disgusted. He'd known all along that Amanda wasn't too crazy about having a bunch of stepsisters and brothers. She'd made that pretty clear from the beginning. So to find out that one of them was a coward naturally wouldn't exactly make her happy. He didn't blame her. It didn't make him very happy either.

The rest of the way home he felt really rotten, and just as they got to the house, Amanda did something that made him feel even rottener.

It happened right after they came through the back door into the kitchen. David was taking off his backpack when he looked up and noticed that Amanda was looking at him.

"Well," she said. "That was an interesting hike." Then she halfway closed her eyes, nodded and said, "Very interesting." And then she smiled at him. She'd smiled at him before, of course. Not very often, but enough so that he knew what it usually looked like, and this was different.

It didn't take him long to figure it out. What it was, was

that she felt sorry for him. All of a sudden he knew that that was it. And that made him feel rottener than anything.

So the way it turned out, the hike that was supposed to take his mind off his problems only gave him another one to worry about. Now—besides the fight he might have to have with Garvey, and the fight that Dad and Molly were probably having—there was the fact that Amanda was sorry for him. It was all pretty depressing.

After Amanda left, David started unpacking his backpack. He'd about finished when he heard something in the pantry. Thinking that it must be mice again—like most old houses the Westerly House seemed to attract mice—he tiptoed over to the door. When he jerked it open, there was a squeaking noise—but it wasn't a mouse.

It was Esther who had squeaked, but Janie was there, too. Still dressed in their party dresses, both Esther and Janie were staring at David with wide eyes and trying to hide something behind their backs.

"Okay, what are you guys up to now?" David said.

"We're not swiping anything," Janie said. "We're just fixing some stuff from the party. See." She brought a great big greasy-looking paper bag out from behind her. "Show him, Tesser," she said, and Esther produced a pie pan full of a melted looking mess with a couple of birthday cake candles sticking out of the top. "See," Janie said. "Mrs. Calder gave everyone so much cake and ice cream that a lot of people left stuff on their plates. So we decided to keep it from going to waste."

Esther nodded proudly and pointed to the paper bag. "See." she said. "We made a doggy bag."

54

"No," Janie shouted. "You idiot, Tesser. I told you! It's not a doggy bag. It's for King Tut. It's a turkey bag."

"A turkey bag?" David said, grinning.

"Well." Janie narrowed her eyes and looked at David speculatively. "Look, David. If we tell you a very, very important secret will you promise, absolutely, positively . . ."

"Don't tell me," David said, closing the door. "I can't handle it."

Chapter
Six

Luckily David slept soundly that night. He'd really expected to have a nightmare or two, or at least to lie awake worrying. It must have been the hike and all the fresh air and exercise that helped him go immediately to sleep and stay that way until Rolor started rattling the door of his cage and squawking for his breakfast. David got up and fed the crow and got back in bed.

Watching Rolor eat reminded him of the huge panful of cake and melted ice cream. Had Janie and Esther really fed it to King Tut—or to what? David told himself he didn't want to know. He had enough problems without having to worry about the kids doing exactly what they'd promised not to—encouraging Blair to take his fantasies seriously. But still, he couldn't help being a little curious about why they'd brought home all those birthday party leftovers. He kept putting it out of his mind but it kept coming back, and finally he wound up doing a little investigating.

It was right after breakfast and David was on his way to the garage when he heard King Tut gobble. Before he was even sure what was in his mind, David found himself strolling over to the turkey pen. "Hey, Tut," he said, sticking his finger through the wire mesh. "How'd you like the birthday cake?"

The turkey blinked his round blank eyes and bobbed his head up and down on its long scraggly neck, making himself look even dumber than usual. David grinned. He was glad Molly had saved Tut from the roasting pan. The way things had been going lately, it was nice to have someone in the family who was more of a turkey than he was. He looked around the pen. There was no sign of the pie pan, but then the kids could have taken it away. Or—they might have left it somewhere else in the first place. Like on the bench by the swing tree.

Actually it was an oak, but the kids had always called it "the swing tree." A rubber tire swing hung from one of its thick branches and a decrepit circular bench went clear around its trunk. The pie pan was on the bench, and it was empty. Empty and very clean, as if it had been washed, or maybe—licked. David was still wondering if a raccoon or maybe Rocky, the barn cat, could have licked it that clean, when right behind him a deep gravelly voice said, "Sixty-three." It was Mr. Golanski.

Mr. Golanski was an old farmer and handyman who lived on a little ranch about a mile up Fillmore Road. He'd lived in the same house ever since he was born; his father, who'd been a carpenter and woodcarver, had worked for the Westerlys. It was Mr. Golanski who had first told the Stanleys about the poltergeist that, it was said, haunted the Westerly House back in the eighteen nineties. That poltergeist had supposedly been stirred up by Henriette, who was a teenager and lived in the house at the time. Talking to Mr. Golanski was always like coming in on the middle of a conversation— even when he didn't sneak up behind you first.

"Hi," David said, when he'd finished almost jumping out of his shoes. "Sixty-three what?"

"Sixty-three years old."

Mr. Golanski was carrying a gun. A huge heavy-looking gun with two barrels. David stared at it. "Oh," he said, nodding. It took him a minute to get his mind off the gun, but when he did it occurred to him that maybe Golanski meant it was his birthday. He was starting to say "congratulations," when he noticed that Golanski was pointing. "Ohhh. You mean the tree?"

Mr. Golanski drew his bushy eyebrows together into a white hedge that ran clear across his face. "The tree," he said sternly, "is much older than sixty-three. The bench is sixty-three years old. I watched my father build it when I was very young. Where is your father?"

David went to the back door and called, and in a minute Dad came out, followed by the whole family. Golanski was such a weird old character that people tended to be curious, and Janie, David suspected, had some kind of tall tale going about him, because she and the twins never lost an opportunity to stare at him.

Mr. Golanski wouldn't come inside even though Molly

invited him in to have breakfast. "Breakfast?" he said, frowning and looking up at the sun. He didn't say it was too late to be eating breakfast, but he might as well have. "I want only a moment of your time," he said to Dad. "There is something you should be told."

But when Dad asked him what it was, Golanski only frowned his famous bushy frown and jerked his head toward the kids. "In private," he said. So Dad asked them all to go back in the house, which obviously bugged Molly and made everybody extremely curious—particularly Janie, who left very slowly with her head turned so far around backwards that she looked like an owl. As soon as she got into the kitchen, she ran to the sink, and climbed up on it and stared out the window, as if she thought she could read Mr. Golanski's lips. The minute Dad came back into the house, everybody pounced.

"Hey, wait a minute," Dad said. "Stand back. Give me air. I'll tell—every word—I promise. Mr. Golanski seemed to feel that what he had to say was too frightening for the tender ears of women and children, but he obviously lives in the far distant past. Ears in general have toughened since his heyday, and in this particular family . . ."

At that point nearly everybody interrupted at once. "Jeff," Molly began—and then everybody was saying things like, "Okay, okay," and "Ears—schmears." And louder than anybody else Janie was yelling, "What did he say? Why did he have a gun? What did he say?"

"All right," Dad said. "All right. Quiet! That's better. It seems that Mr. Golanski has been having trouble with thieves. He's lost a few chickens, and things have been disappearing from his spring house. Milk and cream and ham and once an entire pig carcass. He's convinced that the culprits are escaped prisoners. It seems some prisoners escaped from a conservation camp somewhere up in the Fillmore Hills, and there was some reason to think they headed this way."

"Oh yes," Molly said. "I think I heard something about it on the radio just this morning."

"Yeah," Amanda said. "Some of the kids were talking about it at school. They said a police helicopter had been flying around looking for them."

"For goodness sake," Molly said. "So that's what they were doing. A helicopter flew over here several times, while you were all at school. Friday morning, I think it was. It kept going back and forth right over the house, or at least that's what it sounded like." Molly looked a little worried.

"Escaped prisoners!" Janie's eyes had their high-frequency gleam and her tone of voice was the one a normal kid would use to say "a free trip to Disneyland" or something. Dad shook his head.

"Now look here, Janie. This not a game. I don't think for a minute that Mr. Golanski is right about the prisoners hiding out near here, but if they were, it would be a serious and possibly dangerous thing. And just to be on the safe side we're going to take some precautions. It might be best if there were no more hikes in the hills until this thing is settled. And we'll all have to be extra careful about keeping everything locked up."

Esther began to whimper and say she was scared.

"There's no need to be frightened," Dad said. "Those

prisoners could be clear across the country by now, and they probably are. David, you and Amanda were up in the hills yesterday. You didn't see any signs of campfires or anything like that did you? Any signs of someone hanging around?"

David opened his mouth and then closed it. If anyone questioned Pete Garvey about being out in the hills near Golanski's place, he would know immediately who had told. Dad looked at David questioningly, and he was still opening and closing his mouth when Amanda said, "Well, we did see some dirt bikers, in a big valley not far from Golanski's place. But I don't think they'd steal his stuff. Not milk and pigs, anyway."

"Yeah," David said, gratefully. "If he was missing stuff like tools and gasoline it would be different, but I don't think those guys are interested in food."

Dad grinned. "Well, I certainly don't understand people who go out and destroy virgin land with those contraptions, but I imagine they're human. I suspect they get hungry, just like anyone else."

"Yeah. I guess so," David said, "but I just don't think . . ."

"Couldn't it have been an animal?" Amanda asked.

"I asked Mr. Golanski about that," Dad said. "It seemed quite possible to me, particularly since the thieves apparently strike at night. But he said the spring house door was latched, and the milk and cream disappeared from pans on a high shelf. The ham and the pig carcass were cut down from where they were hanging from rafters. He's sure no animal could have done it."

"Well," Janie said cheerfully, "if it wasn't an animal or

the dirt bikers, it must have been those escaped convicts. I'll bet it was escaped convicts. I'll bet they're hiding in the woods, and when they get hungry, they just go to someone's house and steal food. They're probably going to try to steal our food, too."

Molly rolled her eyes and said, "Bless you, child. You're such a comfort." And Dad said, "Okay, Janie, cool it."

The discussion ended at that point, but David went on thinking about it, trying to make up his mind whether animals, Garvey and his friends, or escaped convicts were the most likely suspects.

He was still thinking about the spring house mystery that afternoon while he worked at the carpenters' bench in the garage. It was a neat place to work. The bench itself, with its shelves and drawers and tool pegs, had been built by Mr. Golanski's father a long time ago, and when the Stanleys bought the house a lot of old tools were still there. David had done quite a bit of building since they'd moved in. Small things mostly, like bird houses and benches, but the tree house was going to be his masterpiece. At the moment he was working on some eight-sided windows for it. He'd sketched out a pattern, measured the boards, mitered the corners, clamped the first piece in the vise and was starting to saw. The saw was old and needed sharpening, so the sawing took a long time. As he worked, David found himself going over the whole thing about the spring house robbers for about the dozenth time.

After considering all the possibilities again, he was beginning to lean toward Garvey and the dirt bikers. He'd really meant it when he told Dad he didn't think they'd be interested in stealing food, but on second thought he could see how it could have happened. They could have stayed late in the valley riding their bikes, until it got dark and they got hungry. And then, instead of going on home, they could have decided to stay and have a barbecue—with Mr. Golanski providing the pork chops. He wouldn't put it past them. And it certainly wouldn't have been very difficult.

David had been to Mr. Golanski's farm several times, and he remembered the spring house. Dad had asked Mr. Golanski to show it to David and the other kids because it was, Dad said, a relic of the past. Instead of having a refrigerator for his cream and cheese and butter, Mr. Golanski had this little stone house built into the side of a hill where a spring of cold water came out of the ground. Inside, it was always very cool and smelled faintly of milk. As David recalled, the thick heavy door was only fastened by an old-fashioned wooden latch. It would have been a cinch for Pete and his dirt biking friends.

As the saw bit slowly through the hard wood, David was picturing it all in his mind—evening shadows, crouching figures creeping silently across the barnyard, the raspy squeak of the spring house door, the narrow beam of a flashlight playing on Pete Garvey's wide flat face . . .

"Hey," somebody said. David looked up, right into the same face, staring in at him from the garage door. For just a fraction of a second he wasn't sure it was real—as if, by thinking about him, he'd somehow conjured up an imaginary Garvey. But then the face opened its mouth and a familiar voice said, "Hi-ya, Stanley." It was Pete Garvey in the flesh.

Chapter
Seven

Garvey was smiling. Even standing as he was with his back to the light, it was clear that the expression on his face was definitely a smile. The chipped tooth gleamed in the front of the mouth, and the lips were curved way up at the corners. Not that it mattered. Garvey always smiled while he was punching people out. "Hi," David said warily.

"I got a flat tire," Garvey said.

David hadn't even noticed the bicycle until then. It looked old and rusty and a lot too little for a guy as huge as Garvey. As he pushed it forward, it made a clunking noise. As Garvey came toward him, David tried to make up his mind whether to run for it or not.

"What are you doing here, Garvey?" Amanda was standing in the entrance to the garage.

Garvey whirled around, swinging the bicycle as if it were light as a feather. "Hi-ya," he said. "I got a flat tire."

Amanda walked around Garvey and the bicycle in a wide circle. When she was standing beside David, she said, "Yeah? So what?"

"I was riding to town only my tire went flat. Right out in front of your place. I just came in to borrow a pump. You got a pump?" Garvey's grin was wider than ever, but something about the way he was talking sounded phony, as if he were reciting lines from a play.

"Not me," Amanda said. She was giving Garvey the look David called her "Medusa special." Guaranteed to turn its victim into stone, or at least into a stuttering klutz. An icy voice went with the stare. "Have you got a pump, David?"

"I'll get it." Still keeping his eyes on Garvey, David sidled along the bench to where he kept his bicycle stuff. He had started back when Amanda grapped the pump out of his hand and headed toward Garvey. Suddenly David was angry. She was treating him as if he were a helpless baby who had to be protected.

"Hey," he said, trying to take the pump back. Amanda held the pump up high with one hand and pushed him so hard with the other that he stumbled and almost fell down. She went on, holding the pump over her head.

"Take it easy," Garvey said. He turned loose of the bike with one hand and tried to move around to the other side, so it would be between him and Amanda. The front wheel began to swivel, and the bike slid sideways. Garvey hopped and stumbled and stepped into the spokes of the front wheel.

65

When he lifted his foot and shook it, the whole bicycle came, too. Then the other wheel swung around and hit him on the back of the leg, and he stumbled backwards and sat down on the bicycle.

Amanda laughed first. David had been trying not to, but when Amanda started, he couldn't help himself. But even while he was laughing he was thinking, This is it—now he's going to murder me, for sure.

Garvey got up slowly and pulled his foot out of the spokes. Then he lifted the bike by the handle bars and held it out in front of him. The spokes in the front wheel looked like a bunch of spaghetti and the rim of the back wheel was obviously crooked. After a while he began to grin.

When Amanda finally stopped laughing, she said she guessed he wouldn't be needing the pump, and Garvey said no he guessed he wouldn't, and then he stood around awhile more, still smiling in a strange way and not saying much. After several more very weird moments, he said he guessed he'd better go, and started off down the drive pushing what was left of the bicycle. But a minute later he turned around and came back.

"Hey, Davey," he said. "Guess I'll just leave this old wreck here 'til tomorrow. Maybe I'll come by after school and try to fix it up. Looks like you got lots of tools and stuff. I'll come by tomorrow. Okay?"

"Well, okay," David said uncertainly.

Pete Garvey trudged off down the road. David and Amanda stood at the garage entrance and watched him go.

"I don't believe it," Amanda said.

"That's exactly what I was thinking," David said. There was something very phony about the whole thing. The strange stiffness of Garvey's smile, for instance, and the way he'd talked, like a bad actor reciting lines. And the whole thing about the bicycle. Garvey just wasn't the bicycle type. A dirt bike or motorcycle, sure, but not a spindly little old rusty one-speed. David went over to where Garvey had left the bike, leaning against the wall. The front tire was flat all right—he hadn't been lying about that. But then David made a discovery. The back tire was flat, too. Obviously, Garvey was lying when he said he was riding by on his way to town when he just happened to get a flat tire. Unless he'd gotten two at the same time—if you could believe that. David didn't.

There was no doubt about it. The whole thing was some kind of phony set-up. Garvey was up to something, and you didn't have to think very hard to figure out what it was. Since he hadn't had any luck catching David at school, he'd decided to get him at home. He'd probably dug up some old wreck of a bicycle that hadn't been ridden in years and pushed it all the way to the Westerly House, to use as an excuse to come in the yard. He'd probably planned to ask David to help him, and then wait for a chance to get him alone. And his plan would have worked perfectly if Amanda hadn't happened to show up.

Earlier that very day David had been considering riding the bus to school again. It had been almost a week since the fiasco in Mrs. Baldwin's class. It seemed as if that should be time enough for someone with an attention span as short as Garvey's to have lost interest in wasting any one particular person. Especially if that person had managed to be as inconspicuous as David had been. But now it seemed that Garvey was not only still after him, but was determined enough to go to a lot of trouble. Not only the trouble to think up the bicycle scheme, which must have put a lot of strain on his mental ability, but also to walk—pushing a wreck of a bike— all the way from his parents' chicken ranch to the Westerly House. It was pretty depressing. After dinner David went out and oiled his bicycle.

The next day was warm and sunny, and David got a specially early start on the ride to school. He got in and out of Mrs. Baldwin's class without any trouble, except that Garvey seemed to be trying to catch his eye all the time. Whenever he did, he gave David a big, wide, leering smile. He was obviously trying to get something across, and it didn't take much imagination to figure out what it was. David didn't like to think about it.

At noon that day in the cafeteria everybody at the table was talking about the escaped convicts. Jerry Murphy's father was a sheriff's deputy, and Jerry had listened in on some of his father's phone conversations and gotten a lot of new information. It seemed that there had been a work crew from the prison who were building a firebreak on Curry Mountain, and one night two of the prisoners had overpowered a guard, stolen his gun and escaped. The sheriff's bloodhound had followed their trail down to the Fillmore foothills. The bloodhound had even located a campsite where it looked as if they'd stayed for a while. But that had been a couple of days ago, and since that time the sheriff and his men hadn't had any luck.

"Something went wrong with the sheriff's dog," Jerry said. "Right after he found the campfire, he was circling around, hit a scent and went tearing off through the woods baying like crazy. My dad and the other guys started running after him, and all at once he came barrelling back kiyiing like a scared puppy. After that he just wouldn't try anymore. Whenever they take him out there to the woods, he just sits down and shivers."

"Hey," David said. "I'll bet he found the prisoners and they did something to him. Like beat him or kicked him, so now he's afraid to find them again. Did he have any wounds or anything?"

"No," Jerry said. "But my dad thinks something like that happened. He thinks they must have done something to him to scare him so bad."

"Hey, Stanley," a guy named Bob Alquist said. "You guys live in that old house out on Westerly Road, don't you? That old house way out there by itself near the Fillmore Hills? Boy, I wouldn't want to live out there right now."

"Yeah," David said in an unconcerned tone of voice. "We're been taking precautions. Since we heard about it we've been locking everything up at night."

Everybody at the table looked at David as if they were really impressed that he was so cool about the whole thing.

"Actually," David said, "on Saturday I went out scouting around in the hills behind our place. You know, just to be sure. I didn't see any sign of them though."

"Sure you did," Jerry said.

"It's the truth," David said, "believe it or not." It was, too. He had been out in the hills on Saturday. He didn't see the need to mention that Amanda had been with him, or that he hadn't really heard about the escaped prisoners until afterwards.

That afternoon when David pedaled, tired and sweaty, into the driveway, Janie was sitting on the front steps. Janie had always been small for her age, and sitting there alone on the broad veranda steps with her back very straight and her hands folded in her lap, she looked like an underdeveloped Barbie doll. The minute he saw her, an automatic Janie alarm went off like a silent siren. The thing was, he'd learned from long experience that when Janie looked particularly cute and harmless, it paid to be on your toes. The minute she saw him she jumped up and came running down the driveway.

"Hi, David," she yelled as he climbed off his bike. "I've been waiting for you."

"What for?" he asked suspiciously. With Janie it paid to be suspicious.

"I want to interview you," Janie said. "I've already interviewed Amanda, and now I want to interview you." She took a little note book and a pencil out of the pocket of her jeans and folded back a page.

"Sure," David said, grinning. "I'm always glad to give interviews to my loyal fans. What do you want to know? How many millions I make? How it feels to be famous?"

"David," Janie said patiently, "don't be dumb. I'm solving the mystery of the escaped prisoners. I want to know if you saw any clues Saturday."

"Oh that!" David had a sudden sinking feeling. He wondered exactly how much Amanda had told about their hike. Like, had she mentioned that she'd come to David's rescue by punching Pete Garvey in the nose. "What did Amanda tell you?" he asked.

Janie turned back a few pages in her notebook. "Well. She told me about seeing squirrels and things and some dirt bikers. She didn't see anything very suspicious, I guess. But I thought you might have noticed something. You're usually pretty good at noticing things."

David breathed a secret sigh of relief. "Sure. I can give you a clue or two," he said. "Just let me get something to eat first. I'm starving."

So Janie followed him into the kitchen, and in between mouthfuls of milk and cookies David made up a few broken twigs and blurry footprints just to keep Janie happy. Then he started telling about the things Jerry had told him at lunch. While he was talking, Amanda came into the kitchen and sat down and listened. He went over all the stuff about the freaked-out bloodhound and how Bob Alquist had said he was glad he didn't live where the Stanleys did. Janie looked excited and wrote very fast. Amanda frowned.

"That's gross," she said. "I wish they'd hurry up and catch those creeps."

David had just taken another cookie when somebody knocked loudly on the backdoor and there was Pete Garvey, leering in at him through the screen. In all the excitement about the prisoners he'd almost forgotten that Garvey had said he was going to come over. Besides he hadn't really believed it. Even Garvey wouldn't be dumb enough to tell his intended victim exactly where and when he was planning to make his next assassination attempt.

"Hi," Garvey said. "I come to work on my bike." He leaned forward and peered through the screen. "Hi," he said to Amanda.

"You again," Amanda said.

Garvey's hand was on the door handle, and he was beginning to open it, so David said, "Come on in."

It was all really weird. David offered Garvey a cookie, and he sat down at the kitchen table and ate six, and drank about a quart of milk. Right at first, nobody but Janie said anything. Garvey ate cookies, Janie rattled on about the escaped prisoners, and David and Amanda just sat there. But after a while Garvey asked David a question about where Janie got that stuff about the bloodhound, and David told him about Jerry's inside information. Before long they were all talking about it. All four of them were still sitting there when Dad came home.

David introduced Garvey, and Dad shook hands and started asking Garvey friendly questions and calling him Pete. David listened, wondering what Dad would say if he knew the truth—if David had introduced Garvey by saying, "This is Pete Garvey, Dad. He just dropped by to punch me out." Instead Dad went on finding out just where the Garvey's poultry farm was and showing a lot of interest in the fact that David's "good old buddy Pete" had just hiked over to see if David could help him repair his bicycle. It wound up with Dad insisting on going out to the garage to inspect the wrecked bicycle and offer his advice on how to put it back together.

Amanda stayed in the house. David guessed that she felt he was safe enough with Dad there, so she didn't have to play bodyguard this time. When Garvey rolled out the pitiful wreck, Dad looked it over and said it was going to have to have some new spokes—which was fairly obvious—but that he thought it could probably be repaired. What he actually said was he didn't think it was a terminal case.

"Terminal?" Garvey said. "No sir. It's a genuine Schwinn."

Dad turned his back quickly and started checking out the back wheel. Then he lifted the bike up on the carpenter's bench and started showing David how to put the wheel in the vise and straighten out the rim. It didn't take very long, but before they were finished Garvey said he thought he'd better be getting home. That was the good news. The bad news was that he also said he was coming back.

"I'll get me some new spokes and come back over in a day or two. If that's all right with you," he said.

"With me?" David said. "Oh, sure."

"Great," Garvey said. "Good-bye, Mr. Stanley." Then he came over to David and stuck out his hand with the palm up. "So long, Davey," he said.

David stared at the hand for a minute before he realized that Garvey was waiting for him to slap it. So he did.

"So long—uh—Pete," he said.

Chapter Eight

The next day when David got home from school, Janie was lying in wait for him again, this time in the kitchen. She obviously had something new up her sleeve, and he guessed right away that it probably wasn't going to be as simple as answering a few questions. She had gone to too much trouble. There was already a glass of milk on the table, and she had a pan of cinnamon toast all ready to go under the broiler.

"Hi David," Janie said with one of her suspiciously cute smiles. "How would you like some cinnamon toast. I made some especially for you." Cinnamon toast happened to be one of his favorite foods. He didn't ask any questions. Whether he asked or not, he was going to find out what she wanted sooner or later. Sooner, probably, he thought, grinning—and he was right. What Janie wanted was for him to take her for a ride on his bicycle.

"Look, Janie," he said. "Ride it yourself. I'm tired."

"I can't. My legs are too short. I just want to go for a little ride. It won't take long."

David sighed. He would have said no, except that by then he'd already eaten most of the cinnamon toast. "Well okay," he said. "Come on then. Let's get it over with."

Out in the garage he stuffed some rags in his book bag and fastened it on the bag rack to make a seat, while he warned Janie to keep her feet out away from the spokes and not to expect a long ride, because it wasn't going to be one. Janie kept bouncing up and down on the tips of her toes the way she always did when she was excited. Then she climbed up behind him, took hold of his belt and said, "All right, let's go. Here we go. This is fun, David. This is so much fun." And then, as they got to the end of the driveway, "No. No, turn left, David. Turn left!"

That should have clued him in, but it really didn't. It wasn't until she'd insisted on turning off Westerly Road onto Fillmore Lane and then kept saying "just a little farther" every time he suggested going back, that he began to catch on to what she had in mind. They were almost to Mr. Golanski's driveway before she admitted it.

"I have to interrogate Mr. Golanski," she said. "I just have to. He probably knows more clues than anybody. He probably saw all kinds of clues in the spring house."

David groaned. Janie and her crazy manias. He'd thought it was bad before—like when she was six years old and preparing for a career as a witch or vampire bat—or like in Italy when she got hung up on Romeo and Juliet and went around practicing various kinds of tragic deaths. But that was before he found out what having a detective in the family could do to your peace of mind.

"Good luck," he said. "I'll wait here." He didn't think it would be necessary to tell her to hurry. Mr. Golanski wasn't the kind to waste much time answering ridiculous questions. He'd probably just growl something unintelligible and throw her out. He thought of trying to warn her and decided against it. Janie could take care of herself. He grinned. In fact, maybe what he ought to do was run ahead and warn Golanski.

Janie pulled her notebook out of her pocket and disappeared down the driveway, as David settled down in the grass beside the road. He'd give her about five minutes, he told himself. Twenty minutes later he got up and went tooking for her.

It didn't take him long to realize that Mr. Golanski wasn't at home. No one answered when he knocked on the front door, and the beat-up old pickup truck wasn't in the garage. So if Janie hadn't been interviewing Mr. Golanski for the last twenty minutes, what in the world had she been doing? He stood on the front porch for a minute or two, feeling more and more uneasy, before it suddenly dawned on him where she was.

There was no one in the cluttered back yard with its jumble of pens and sheds. A bunch of King Tut's relatives, along with some chickens and ducks, raised their heads to stare at him as he went by, and a couple of beige-colored cows leaned over a fence and followed him with their soft deerlike eyes. He was halfway down the path that led toward the hill when Janie suddenly appeared running toward him.

"Come on, David," she said impatiently as if he'd been keeping her waiting. "Come on. I need you."

"Look," he said. "I'm not going in that spring house with you. What if Golanski comes home and catches us in there. He'd probably get out that shotgun of his and shoot first and ask questions afterward." But Janie was tugging on his hand and, besides, he couldn't help being a little bit curious. Looking back over his shoulder now and then, he let her drag him the rest of the way to the spring house.

"Come on," she kept saying. "You have to help me."

The air was damp and cool, and the constant trickling sound that he remembered from his previous visit still came from the corner where the spring water flowed out of the rocky hillside and fell into a deep, clear pool. The air smelled of cream and bacon, and even with the door open behind them the light was very dim. Janie grabbed hold of David's arms.

"Lift me up," she said. "Lift me up. Over there. By those shelves."

With David holding her up as high as he could, Janie leaned forward and peered at the broad shelf that ran around three sides of the spring house. There were pans on the shelf —perhaps a dozen wide shallow pans full of cream-covered milk. Holding on to the edge of the shelf, Janie pulled herself and David down to the corner and partway along the back wall. Once or twice she leaned farther forward and made a gasping noise.

"What is it?" he asked. "What do you see?" But she didn't answer.

Finally she said, "Okay. Put me down," and slid out of

his arms. She was very quiet as he pulled the heavy door shut, turned the latch and hurried her down the path toward the house. Expecting to see Mr. Golanski bursting out of the back door with his gun at any moment, he didn't take time out to ask questions. But their luck held, and they made it safely around the house and down the drive to the bicycle. As Janie climbed on to the book rack, he asked, "What did you see? What did you see on the shelves?"

Janie didn't say anything, so he asked again. After another long pause she said, "Nothing. I didn't see anything."

"Yes, you did," David yelled as he started off down the driveway. He glanced back at her over his shoulder, and she looked up at him with a very strange expression on her face. It was almost as if she were frightened, or at least very worried. Janie didn't frighten easily, and seeing her look that way gave him an uneasy feeling. He stared at her until she suddenly yelled, "Look out," and he turned the handle bars just in time to keep from running into a ditch. After that he decided to wait to give her the third degree until they were safely home. But as soon as they were, he was going to find out what she'd seen in the spring house—or know the reason why.

He didn't, though. As soon as he'd braked the bicycle to a stop in the garage, she jumped off the back and started running toward the house. By the time he caught up with her, she was in the kitchen with Molly; and for the rest of the evening she stayed about two feet from either Molly or Dad, where David was not about to bring up the subject of prowling around on Mr. Golanski's property. It wasn't until almost bedtime that he trapped her in the upper hall and dragged her into his room.

"Hey, let me go," she yelled.

"Not until you tell me what you saw in the spring house."

She glared at him. "I told you. I didn't see anything."

"You did, too. I heard you make a gasping noise, like you'd seen something very important."

"No. No, I didn't." She glared, and he glared back. And then suddenly she smiled. "David, I was just playing. You know. I was playing detective, and I was pretending I was finding all these important clues like fingerprints and blood-spots and everything. That's all it was. Playing."

"I don't believe you," he said, but actually he wasn't certain. Janie pretended a lot. "If you were just playing, I really ought to wring your neck. I mean, if you got me to sneak around on someone else's property when they weren't home and risk getting my head shot off, just so you could play some silly make believe game . . ."

"David," Janie said. "If you don't let me go you're going to be sorry."

"I will not."

"Yes you will. I have to go to the bathroom."

So that was the end of the discussion, and David didn't know anymore than when he'd started out. It really frustrated him. And one of the most frustrating things about it was that there was no one to discuss it with. He obviously couldn't tell Dad or Molly, and there was no point in trying to talk to the twins about it. Blair probably would just listen and not say anything, and Esther would forget she'd promised not to and tell everybody in sight. That left only Amanda.

He'd never had what you would call a close relationship with Amanda. In fact, it was hard to say just what kind of a relationship they did have, because it was so changeable. They'd had some good times together now and then, like the other day on the hike before Garvey showed up. When Amanda was in one of her better moods, she could be a lot of fun to be around. But he could remember more fights than good times. Fights that went all the way from an exchange of minor insults to a hard crack on the head with whatever weapon was handy. On his head, usually, not Amanda's. In general, she wasn't the kind of person with whom you deliberately shared sensitive information. But that night, not long after he'd given up on Janie, David found himself telling the whole story to Amanda.

They were in the dining room, doing their homework. It happened to be one of the rare times when there was something Dad called "vaguely worth seeing" on television so he wasn't in his usual reading spot. David was halfway through his science report when all of a sudden he found himself telling Amanda all about what happened at Golanski's.

"Man!" she said when he had finished. "That was taking a chance. I'd hate for that old troll to catch me in his spring house."

"Yeah, I know. But I guess I really thought that Janie had found something out—about the escapees, I mean."

Amanda gave him a funny look. "Sure, but she could

have gotten you both shot, the little maniac—just so she could play one of her idiotic games."

He shrugged. "You think that's all it was then? Just a game?"

"Sure. If she'd really found something out, why wouldn't she tell? I mean if she'd seen a clue the thieves had left there, or something like that, why wouldn't she tell you about it?"

"I guess you're right," David said. It made sense. It was just that, knowing Janie as well as he did, he was pretty familiar with all her acts, and he somehow felt she hadn't been pretending about being worried when they left the spring house. But when he tried to explain the feeling to Amanda, she said, "Sure she was worried. She'd just realized what you were going to do to her when you found out it was all just a dumb game."

David nodded. "What do you think about the prisoners?" he asked. "Do you think they're still around?"

"Me?" She grinned at David. "Well—let me run upstairs and see if I can find my old crystal ball and I'll let you know all about it." She laughed sarcastically and went back to her geometry. She usually laughed when anyone mentioned supernatural stuff, since she'd stopped being interested in it herself.

They both went on working for a few minutes, but then, all of a sudden, Amanda looked up. "I wish they'd catch those guys," she said in a very serious tone of voice. "I don't like to think about them being around here. I've been dreaming about it. About people staring in the windows at us at night when we're sitting around like this, or breaking into the house after we've all gone to bed." She glanced toward the window and raised her shoulders in a kind of shudder. "It really scares me. You don't seem to be very scared, but it really scares me."

"I'm scared sometimes," David said, and as soon as he'd said it, he wished he hadn't, because he knew it would remind Amanda of how she'd had to rescue him from Garvey. Sure enough, she looked up and gave him the same strange smile—as if she were sorry for him. For just a moment they stared at each other, and then at the same instant they both looked away. They did the rest of their homework in a stiff embarrassed silence.

The next day Pete Garvey showed up at the house after school again. It was a nice warm day, and David was working on the tree house and all three of the little kids were helping him. He'd rigged up a rope and pulley, and when he needed another board or a special tool the kids would tie it to the rope and he'd wind it up. He was just trying to fit a board in beside one of the windows when he heard Garvey's voice saying, "Hey Davey; I got the spokes."

David groaned inwardly. Then he said, "Hi," and explained that he wanted to finish the window first. He wasn't about to go into the garage alone with old Pete if he could help it. Three little kids weren't much protection, but at least they were witnesses, and that might discourage Garvey a little bit. He stood around at the foot of the tree watching for a few minutes, and then he climbed up and offered to help.

Fortunately there was only one hammer and David had it. Pete helped by holding boards in place while David nailed them, and whether it was the hammer, or the little kids, or what, he didn't actually do anything violent. He threatened to, however. Once when he was holding a board he said, "Watch it, Davey. You clobber my fingers with that hammer and I'll stuff you out the window." But he didn't actually try to do it, and after a while David began to relax a little.

He was actually thinking that maybe Pete had given up on punching him out, but then Amanda came out of the house and right away he quit helping and got down out of the tree. So he probably was planning something and only gave up when David's stepsister/bodyguard appeared on the scene. Watching through the eight-sided window, David saw Pete kind of sidle up toward Amanda, moving easy-kneed as if he were getting ready to jump if she started anything. He couldn't hear what they were saying, but they talked for several minutes before Amanda went back in the house.

After she left, Garvey took his spokes and went into the garage, but he couldn't have gotten much done because just a few minutes later he came out and said he had to leave.

"See you later, Davey," he yelled.

Up in the tree, with a hammer in his fist, David suddenly saw the humor in the whole thing. "Not if I see you first, Petey," he yelled back.

Garvey turned around and the chipped tooth shone in the middle of the famous Garvey smile—the smile that looked just the same when he was slapping you on the back or punching you in the mouth. Maybe he'd given up on doing a number on David Stanley and maybe he hadn't. David wasn't counting on it.

Chapter
Nine

On Thursday the police helicopter flew over the school during the lunch hour, and everybody started talking about the escaped prisoners again.

By now everybody knew their names and what they looked like and just how dangerous they were supposed to be. The one the police thought had masterminded the escape was a guy named Herbie "The Weasel" Boston who had been in prison for killing someone in a knife fight. He was the one who particularly interested everyone in Steven's Corners. In the mug shot that appeared in the *Valley Press,* he had a narrow, pinched-looking face with heavy, dark eyebrows and a thin, lipless mouth. The other guy, whose name was Steven Hutter, looked more ordinary, with a fattish face and a short, round nose.

It seemed that when Boston was a kid, he'd lived for a

while in Lucasville, a little town just on the other side of the Fillmore Hills. One man who lived in Steven's Corners even remembered him as a kid. He'd told a lot of people about how mean and vicious The Weasel was, even way back then.

The story was that The Weasel had spent a lot of time exploring the countryside around Lucasville and undoubtedly knew all about the area. That was the reason, everybody said, that he'd managed to hide out for so long and keep ahead of the search parties.

At the middle school, people were calling each other Weasel and making up Weasel jokes. David had become a kind of minor celebrity because he lived way out in the country near the Fillmore Hills. It seemed as if everybody he talked to wanted to ask him if he had seen anything suspicious and to tell him how glad they were they didn't live on Westerly Road.

That evening at the Stanley dinner table the conversation turned out to be more of the same. First Amanda told the latest rumors that were going around at the high school, and then Janie took over with all the wild stories that the kids at the elementary school were coming up with. Just as you might expect, the little kids' stories showed the most originality. One little girl insisted that she'd seen The Weasel roller skating in the park, and somebody in Janie's class had started the rumor that he was holed up in the principal's office and was holding the principal for ransom. Janie insisted that nobody knew who'd started the rumor, but David thought he could make a good guess.

Finally, when David got a chance to talk he started telling about all the attention he'd been getting because of where he lived. But at that point Molly suddenly said she was tired of the whole subject and she didn't want to hear anymore about it.

The next morning, when Dad came down to the breakfast table, he said that he had an announcement to make.

"I was listening to the news while I was dressing," he said, "and it seems we can all start thinking of other subjects for mealtime conversation. Apparently the authorities now believe that The Weasel and his buddy left this area several days ago."

"How do they know?" David asked.

"It seems someone spotted them in Reno."

"Phooey," Janie said. "Now I can't solve the mystery."

Everybody laughed. David felt relieved, mainly, but there was a part of him that felt a little bit like Janie did, but for another reason. He didn't have any silly ideas about solving the case, but he had been enjoying all the extra attention he'd been getting at school. "Did they catch them yet?" he asked Dad.

"No. Not yet, apparently. But they seem to feel it won't be long."

Molly put a bowl of fortified oatmeal on the table and sat down with a big sigh. "Well," she said, "I don't know about the rest of you, but I'm relieved. I didn't say much because I didn't want to frighten you kids, but I've been really nervous about having those thugs right out there practically in our backyard. I've wasted a lot of energy peeking out of windows and listening to strange noises lately, and I'm awfully glad it's all over."

"I think we all are," Dad said. "It's a big load off everyone's mind." He looked at Molly and grinned. "Just in time for the president's reception, too. How about changing your mind about not going?"

They'd all heard about the reception. It was to be at the university and Dad was obliged to be there, but Molly hadn't been planning to go. What she'd been saying was that she just didn't feel in the mood for a big social bash, but when Dad asked her to change her mind she did—in a hurry. Obviously she'd really been worried about going away and leaving the kids alone at night. Actually that was pretty ridiculous. David and Amanda had been doing the baby-sitting for a long time, and it really didn't make much sense for Molly to stay home simply because of the escaped prisoners. If two armed men walked into the house, it wouldn't make a whole lot of difference whether little old Molly was there or not. But now, with the prisoners out of the picture, it was obvious that Molly had really wanted to go to the reception all along.

At school that day there was still a lot of talk about the convicts. Most people said they were glad the men weren't around Steven's Corners anymore, but a few said they were sorry because they were going to miss all the excitement. It was true that Steven's Corners could use something to relieve the monotony, and for a while the convicts had certainly done it. David thought about the difference it had made, and he also wondered how the convicts had managed to get out of the woods and all the way to Reno without being seen. With everybody for miles around on the alert and watching for them, they must have been awfully lucky to have managed it.

When he got home from school, Molly was already getting dressed for the reception, and just before dinnertime she and Dad left. That was about five thirty, and it was only about half an hour later that the announcement came over the radio. David was in the kitchen helping to get dinner ready. Amanda had the radio tuned to a rock and roll station, when someone broke into the music to make a special announcement. The man who'd been identified in Reno as Weasel Boston had been caught and it wasn't The Weasel at all—just someone who looked like him. The authorities had now resumed the search in the Fillmore Hills area.

"Hey, did you hear that?" Janie said. "Goody, goody!"

Amanda looked at David and raised her eyebrows. "It's a good thing Molly didn't hear it."

"Yeah. She'd never have gone tonight if she had."

"I know," Amanda said.

Janie jumped down off the stool where she'd been stirring the meat for tacos and dashed out of the room yelling, "Stir the meat, Tesser. I've got to get my escaped prisoner notes out of the wastepaper basket."

"Well, I'm glad somebody's happy," Amanda said. She didn't sound glad, however. David wasn't exactly pleased, himself. It was beginning to get dark outside, and Dad and Molly were not due home until midnight or later. When Janie came back with her notebook, David told her to put it away.

"We're not going to talk about the prisoners tonight," he told her. "Nobody's going to even mention them. Okay?" He must have sounded like he meant it, because nobody did, at least not until Pete Garvey showed up.

They heard him long before he got to the house. The

gurgly roar of the motor got louder and louder while he was still out on Westerly Road, and when he turned into the driveway, it completely drowned out the sound of the TV. The little kids jumped up and ran to the window.

"Hey," Janie shouted, "it's Pete on a motorcycle."

"Ye gods," David said. "That's all we need."

The little kids dashed for the back door, and David got up slowly and followed. Amanda followed David. When they got to the driveway, Pete was letting Janie try sitting in the seat.

"Where'd you get that thing?" Amanda asked.

"It's Ace's brother's," Pete said. "I borrowed it. I had to bring over the new tubes." He reached in the saddlebag and brought out two new bicycle tubes. "I was going to bring them over earlier, but my dad made me clean out the brooder and I didn't get done in time."

"Don't you have to have to be sixteen and have a license to drive these things?" David asked.

"Naw. Not unless you ride them on roads."

"You had to ride on roads to get over here, didn't you?"

"These little country roads don't matter," Pete said. "Besides I figured all the cops were probably still home resting up."

"Resting up?" Amanda said. She looked at David and then back at Pete. "Haven't you heard?"

He hadn't, and when Amanda told him, he didn't believe her. He parked the motorcycle and came into the house, still arguing that just a few hours ago he'd heard how they were just about to catch the two guys in Reno. And when he finally did believe her, after David and Janie and even Esther insisted that they'd heard the announcement, too, he didn't look too happy about it. He didn't say so, but David wondered if he could be thinking about the long ride back down Westerly Road, alone and in the dark. David was glad he didn't have to do it.

The TV was still going when they got back to the living room, and Pete announced that it was time for his favorite program, so they all sat down and watched *The Dukes of Hazzard*. Dad had researched all the TV shows and rated them on a list that went from "Approved" to "Only Over My Dead Body." The Dukes of Hazzard was way down the list. But since Dad's TV DECREE hadn't covered a situation where you had a guest like Pete Garvey demanding to see something in the "Not A Chance" category, David decided not to mention it. Neither did anyone else.

Janie watched buggy-eyed; Esther hid her head under a pillow; and Blair went to sleep; and when it was over, it was time for the little kids to go to bed. After the kids were gone, Amanda turned on the radio to a rock station, and she and David and Pete listened to music and talked about the prisoner thing. Amanda was telling Pete about the new locks Dad had gotten for the doors and how careful they'd all been lately to lock everything up—when simultaneously, she and David turned and looked at each other.

"The locks," she said.

David nodded and got out of his chair. As he started toward the door, there was a sudden thud, as if something had hit the wall outside the living room.

"What was that?" Pete whispered.

"Just the shutters, I think," David said. "They do that when it's windy." They turned off the radio then and listened. It was windy, all right. The old house was singing its wind-song, a low whistling moan that seemed to come from all directions at once, accompanied by occasional scrapes and rattles when the branches of trees brushed against the outside walls. They listened, looking at the windows.

"The locks," David said finally and started for the hall. He was halfway to the front door when Pete and Amanda caught up with him. They checked the front door and the one that led outside from Molly's studio, both of which were locked, and the kitchen door—which wasn't. David locked it then, carefully—both the old-fashioned key lock and the new dead-bolt—and when he'd finished, Amanda checked it to be sure he'd done it right.

Back in the living room they sat around making short comments in low voices in between long spells of listening to the wind. By then it was eleven o'clock, and David had run out of things to say that Pete showed any interest in. Now and then he seemed not to hear what David was saying at all, as if his mind was on something else, but he still hadn't said anything about going home. Once or twice he got up and went to the window, but that was as far as he went. He'd stared out into the darkness for a few minutes, then come back and sit down.

It was in the middle of a long uncomfortable silence that Amanda suddenly said, "What was that?"

"What was what?" David said.

"Shh. Listen."

They all heard it then, even over the whine of the wind —a raspy clicking noise that obviously was coming from the direction of the kitchen.

"It's probably just Esther raiding the cookie jar," David whispered.

They were still listening tensely when suddenly there was a loud thud that seemed to shake the windows all over the house, and the door to the back hall flew open and banged against the wall. A rush of cold air flowed into the room, rustling the edges of the newspapers on the coffee table. They all sat very still, staring at the door.

"I'm going to see," David said, finally. When he reached the door, he looked back, and Amanda and Pete were right behind him.

The rush of wind got stronger in the hall. The kitchen was like a wind tunnel. And the back door was wide open. The back door that they'd carefully locked and double-locked only a short time before.

David took a step back and bumped into Pete and Amanda. The wind roared in through the open door, and a bunch of paper napkins flew off the table and fluttered around the room like frightened birds.

A high voice that David didn't immediately recognize as Pete's said, "It was locked. You locked it."

"They must have picked it," Amanda whispered. "That's what I heard—them picking it."

"God almighty!" Pete said.

David turned around and looked behind him just as Pete and Amanda did the same thing. Pushing between them, David stepped into the hall and looked up—up the stairs to where the little kids were alone on the second floor. Afterwards he didn't remember what he thought or how he felt at all, or even deciding to do what he did. He just remembered stopping outside Esther and Janie's room for just a second before he opened the door. They were all right—sleeping quietly. He ran down the hall and into his own room and then quickly into and out of all the other upstairs rooms and then back down the stairs. Pete and Amanda were still standing at the hall door.

"It's Blair," David said. "He's gone."

Outside it was pitch black. David stood for a second on the porch in the rushing darkness. Remembering the flashlight Molly kept in the pantry, he dashed back into the kitchen, shoving Pete out of his way as he went in, and again on his way out.

He stopped again on the porch and tried to call, but his voice came out weak and high, and the wind snatched the sound and swallowed it into its constant roar. As he ran down the walk, the darkness around him was alive and moving, as if the wind was a flowing black torrent that caught at his breath and seemed to blur and bend the narrow beam of the flashlight. He looked in the garage and up and down the drive before it came to him—suddenly and with frightening certainty—where he should look next.

In the backyard he glanced toward the swing tree and stopped with a gasp as a swirling shadowy form seem to rise up from the ground and drift toward him. But as he swung around, the ghostly form moved into the beam of light and disintegrated into particles, a whirling mass of dust and dead leaves. He went on, toward the gate to the garden.

He caught sight of Blair's hair the moment he opened the gate. He stopped the swing of the flashlight's beam, brought it back and focused it on Blair's blond head. He seemed to be crouching down close to the ground. Something, a vague movement in the darkness, made David move the light a little to the left—a little to the left and up directly above Blair's head—where two gleaming red eyes turned to stare in his direction. Something—it felt like his heart—rose up and seemed to explode somewhere near the bottom of his throat. The light, moving in his shaking hand, revealed a shadowy outline—an enormous shaggy head and, silvery in the sliding light, the bulk of an enormous body.

"Blair," David's voice broke and quavered. "Come here."

It growled then, a deep threatening rumble, and white fangs glinted beneath the gleaming eyes. As David moved forward, Blair jumped to his feet.

"Don't, David," Blair called. "Stop."

Behind David a voice said, "God almighty."

Chapter Ten

When Blair told David to stop, he did. For just a second he stood perfectly still, but then the thing growled louder and moved closer. Now the white teeth gleamed only a few inches from Blair's face. David moved slowly forward.

"Blair," he called softly. "Back away from him. Move slowly."

David was almost to where he could touch Blair when the low rumble of the growl suddenly rose to a terrifying roar, and the monster lunged forward. Behind David someone screamed. As the enormous animal headed straight for David, Blair threw his arms around the thick neck.

"No, Nightmare," he said. "No. Down. Lie down." It stopped then, and with a growl still rumbling in its throat, it slowly lowered its huge body to the ground. Blair didn't take his arms from around its neck until it was lying down and he was sitting beside it on the ground. With his face close to its ear, he began to talk. The howl of the wind drowned out most of what he was saying, but David heard enough to know that Blair was telling the shaggy monster that it was a good dog and that David was good, and that everything was all right. Then Blair got up again and tugged on the dog's collar, and it got up too.

"Okay, David." Blair's smile glowed in the flashlight's beam. "He knows now. You can pat him now."

David's heart hadn't stopped thundering against his ribs, but suddenly he wasn't at all afraid anymore. In fact the terrible fear he'd been feeling just a moment before was suddenly gone, replaced by a sudden rush of mixed-up emotions —relief and surprise and a really great flash of amazed excitement. Blair's dog was real. A real flesh and blood, warm and alive, and absolutely unbelievably enormous—dog. It didn't seem possible, but it was true. Very slowly he put out his hand—down low and with the palm up.

"Hi, Nightmare," he said in the most calm and reassuring tone of voice he could manage. "Good dog, Nightmare."

The shaggy muzzle moved down and forward until it almost touched David's fingers, and then the long tail stirred slightly in what looked almost like a wag.

A hand grabbed David's arm, and Amanda leaned over his shoulder and said, "Tell him I'm okay, Blair. And Pete. Tell him we're friends, too."

Tipping his head, the way he always did when he was thinking, Blair looked from Amanda to Pete and back again. "Are you going to tell?" he said at last. "Janie says if we tell, they'll take Nightmare away. To the pound, Janie says. You won't tell, will you?"

"Me?" Amanda said. "No. I won't tell. I promise. Absolutely. Totally to the max. What a great, huge, totally outrageous secret! Bleeper honey, I absolutely can't wait not to tell."

"Me too," Pete said. "I don't snitch. Not on dogs or nobody."

Blair nodded slowly. Then he turned his back and put his hand on the side of the dog's head and pulled it around. Standing there, flat-footed, on all four feet, the dog's head was on a level with Blair's. Putting his mouth close to the dog's ear, Blair talked for a while and then turned around to point at Amanda. Then he whispered some more and pointed at Pete. Then he crooked his finger at them. "Come on," he said.

When Nightmare sniffed Amanda's fingers, his tail again stirred slightly. But when Pete stuck his hand out, he only looked at him and growled softly. Pete took his hand away quickly. The dog was still inspecting Amanda and Pete when the garden gate banged open and shut and something ran into David from the rear. It was Janie and Esther, breathless with excitement and, in Janie's case at least, anger.

"Blair," she hissed, "you told. Why did you tell? Now the pound will get him for sure." Janie's face was about an inch from Blair's, and her voice outscreeched the wind. A low rumbling sound came from somewhere deep inside Nightmare's huge chest.

"Shh," Blair said to the dog, and then to Janie, "I didn't

tell. I just brought Nightmare his dinner, and then they came too."

Janie turned to glare at David. "It's the truth," he said. "The wind blew the door open after Blair went out, and we came looking for him. So calm down. And besides, we aren't going to tell. Nobody is."

"Relax, wimp," Amanda said. "We've all promised not to tell. But how on earth have you little wimps managed to hide him all this time?"

"Well," Janie said, "I've been kind of the mastermind. I've been making all the plans about keeping him hidden. Haven't I, Blair?"

Blair nodded. "Janie's been making lots of plans. But we don't hide Nightmare. He hides himself."

Amanda looked at David and grinned. "And what have you been doing?" she said to Esther.

"I'm freezing to death," Esther said. "Let's go inside."

It wasn't until Esther mentioned it that David realized he was cold, too. Very cold, in fact. He'd run outside without a coat or sweater, and now the chill wind seemed to have blown right through his skin and flesh and clear to the center of his bones. "Esther," he said through chattering teeth, "that's the best idea anyone's had yet. Come on, everybody. Come on, Nightmare. Will he come in the house, Blair?"

"I don't know," Blair said. "I'll ask him."

He wouldn't come at first. When they all bunched around him telling him to "come" and "heel" and "Here, boy", he just stood there staring at them. But then Blair tugged at David's arm and whispered that the rest of them should all go on ahead. When David reached the steps, he looked back to see Blair and Nightmare coming across the yard. Blair was holding the dog's collar. They walked side by side across the backyard and up the steps into the kitchen.

In the kitchen Nightmare started growling again until everyone crowded together across the table from him and Blair. In the bright light he looked bigger than ever. Less like a weird shaggy monster, perhaps, and more like a dog, but maybe for that very reason, definitely bigger. The thing was, you don't really know what size to expect in a monster, but you do in a dog, and this dog was definitely beyond all expectations. In some ways it resembled a Great Dane, except it was taller than any Dane David had ever seen, and instead of being smooth-coated, it was covered by a heavy coat of shaggy bristly gray-brown hair. Tufts of gray-brown hair stood up over its large dark eyes in shaggy eyebrows and surrounded its gigantic muzzle like a frizzled beard.

"Wow," David said. "That's some dog."

"That," Amanda said, "is, without a doubt, the biggest dog in the whole world."

"Lordy," Pete said. "What a mutt! I'd sure like to have a mutt like that." He started around the table, but when Nightmare lifted his lip on one side just enough to show a few huge teeth, Pete stopped and backed up.

Blair looked worried. He took hold of Nightmare's lip and pulled it down over the tooth. "He's just nervous," he said. "He's not very used to houses." He cupped his hands over the dog's ear and whispered, and the dog immediately lay down.

"See," Janie said. "Blair talks dog language."

"What did you say to him, Bleeper?" Amanda asked.

"I said 'lie down.' " Blair said.

"Some dog language," Amanda said. "Blair doesn't speak dog language. The dog speaks English."

"Well, he's been trained, anyway," David said.

Eventually, they all settled down where they were, with everyone sitting around one side of the table, except for Blair and Nightmare. Janie and Esther, and now and then Blair, began to tell everything they knew about Nightmare, which turned out to be not a whole lot.

How it started was particularly vague because that part depended on Blair for the telling, and he had never been the greatest at explaining things. It was all pretty confusing, but the gist of the story seemed to be that Blair looked out of the window one night and the dog was in the garden and he was hungry, so Blair went down and found something for him to eat.

Actually what Blair said was, "We went down and found something . . ."

"We?" David asked. "I thought that was before Janie and Esther knew about him."

"Yes," Blair said.

"Then who . . ." David started to ask, when he suddenly knew the answer, even before Esther leaned over and whispered in his ear. Esther was famous for mushy-mouthed whispers, but this time there wasn't much doubt about what she'd said. It was, "Harriette."

David decided Harriette was a complication they didn't need to get into at the moment. "Okay, okay," he said. "What does he eat?"

"Everything," Blair said.

"Lots of everything," Esther burst out. "We feed him lots and lots. Blair told me first, and then we told Janie, and Janie and me been finding lots of stuff for him to eat."

"And I named him," Janie said. "When Blair told me about him, I said he sounded like a nightmare, and Blair through I meant that was the kind of dog he was, so he started calling him Nightmare. But what he really is, is an Irish wolfhound. I looked him up in the encyclopedia at school. He's an Irish wolfhound, and they're the tallest dogs in the world, and they're supposed to look shaggy and kind of bristly like that."

"Hey," Amanda said suddenly, "the bread. Remember David? That's what Blair was doing with the bread. What else have you kids been feeding him? He must eat an awful lot."

"He does," Esther said. "He eats an awful lot of everything. We've been feeding him leftovers and stuff Molly burns and lunches and dog food."

"Lunches?" David asked.

"Sure," Janie broke in. "At school I told everybody our father lost his job and we're very poor now, so everybody's been saving stuff they don't want from their lunches for us."

"Ye gods," David said.

"And once," Janie went on, "when we had enough money, I went to the grocery store during lunch hour and bought a big bag of dog food. Only we couldn't let anybody see it, so we tore the bag open and poured it into our lunch pails."

David vaguely remembered Molly making a fuss about the kids lunch pails a week or so before. "That rings a bell.

Wasn't that when Molly kept asking you why your lunch pails smelled like dead fish?"

"Yes. You're right, David." Janie sounded as if he'd just answered the winning question on a quiz show. "And how about the spring house? Does that ring a bell, too?"

"The spring house?" David was bewildered.

"Yes. Why I wouldn't tell you what I saw there?"

"Don't tell me . . ." David said.

Janie nodded hard. "It was toenail scratches. I was really looking for clues about the escaped prisoners, but when I saw toenail scratches near the latch and along the edge of the shelves, I knew it was Nightmare who took the stuff. Mr. Golanski probably would have guessed, too, except he thought everything was too high up for an animal to reach. But he hasn't seen Nightmare."

"But I still don't understand why you wouldn't tell me," David said.

"Because I thought you'd tell. You always tell Dad everything."

"No, I don't," David said.

"Yes, you do. At least you tell him if he asks," Janie said.

David grinned. "Okay then. We'll just have to make sure he doesn't ask. What we'll have to do is, be sure Dad doesn't just happen to ask if anybody is hiding the world's biggest dog on the premises."

"Real cute, Davey," Amanda said, "but you'd better not tell, no matter what. You know what he said about no more pets. I mean, if your dad wouldn't even consider a few ounces of hamster, what's he going to say about a half-ton of dog?

And besides, if Nightmare really did steal all that stuff from Golanski, he's really in trouble if he gets caught. Golanski will probably insist on shooting him."

Amanda was right. There didn't seem to be any solution except to keep Nightmare a complete secret. Which might have seemed pretty impossible, considering his size, except for the fact that Blair had already been doing it for three or four weeks.

"Where have you been hiding him?" David asked.

"I told you," Blair said. "He hides himself. Janie hid him once, but he didn't stay."

"I put him in the tool shed," Janie said. "But he scratched the door open."

"But how did you keep him from hanging around during the daytime?"

"I just told him," Blair said. "I said not to."

Apparently Nightmare had been coming to the house every night to be fed and then disappearing back into the hills and not showing up again until the next night.

"I don't get it," Pete said. "We get strays around our place sometimes, and if you feed them—man, you got 'em. I mean for good. They don't go off and hide for a minute, leave alone a whole day."

"Hey, I got it," Amanda said. "I'll bet he belongs to somebody else and he goes back there every day. Only they don't feed him enough or something so he comes over here every night to pig out."

Blair shook his head.

"Well," David said, "I don't know. If anybody around here had a dog like that, we'd know about it, wouldn't we?"

"Yeah," Pete said. "I been living out here all my life, and my folks know just about everybody. It don't seem likely anybody'd get a dog like that and not mention it."

They kicked around a few more theories about where Nightmare disappeared to during the day time, including one of Janie's that he was actually a kind of werewolf who turned into a human being as soon as it got light. None of the theories seemed very likely, and by then it was getting dangerously close to the time for Dad and Molly to get home. So when Amanda suggested that they shut Nightmare in the tool shed and padlock the door, everyone more or less agreed.

As soon as the decision was made, everyone swung into action. David went looking for a padlock, Amanda rounded up some old blankets to make a dog bed, and the rest of them went along as Blair coaxed Nightmare into the tool shed. He wouldn't go in at first, even when Blair told him to, and it all took quite a bit of time. They'd barely gotten everyone back into the house and the little kids upstairs to bed, when they heard Dad's car in the driveway.

Dad and Molly looked surprised to find Pete Garvey there at that hour of the night; but before they had time to say anything, David and Amanda started telling them about the prisoners and how they hadn't left the area after all.

Molly said, "Oh no," in a very upset tone of voice, and Dad looked worried and asked some questions about exactly what the announcement had said.

"Well, that is discouraging," he said at last. "I'd thought that was one problem we didn't have hanging over us any longer."

"I thought so too," Pete said. "I thought those guys were

long gone or I sure wouldn't have come all the way over here alone in the dark."

So then Dad offered to drive Pete home, and Pete accepted very quickly, and everyone else went to bed.

David wondered about that for a few minutes—about Pete being nervous about riding home on the motorcycle. It was an interesting thought. It hadn't occurred to him before that a six-foot guy on a cycle could be nervous about anything.

He didn't think about it for long however. What he went to sleep thinking about was the fact that a fantastically enormous dog was actually hidden in the Stanley tool shed. It didn't seem possible. As he got sleepier, it seemed more and more like the whole thing had been a Blair-type fantasy and when he woke up in the morning the dog would be gone.

Actually, it was.

Chapter Eleven

The plan was for David and Blair to get up early and let Nightmare out of the tool shed. They were to feed him and let him exercise—out behind the garage where they couldn't be seen from the house—and then shut him back up. The only trouble was, Blair wouldn't wake up. If Blair had some kind of internal alarm system that went off when Nightmare needed attention, it apparently didn't function at six o'clock in the morning. Finally David gave up and went by himself.

In the kitchen he tiptoed around fixing a pan of leftovers and bread and milk. Outside, the wind had died down to a weak whisper, but the yard was full of reminders of its former power. Dead leaves, twigs and small branches were scattered everywhere. On the way out to the tool shed David wondered what kind of a reception he would get when he opened the door—without Blair there to tell Nightmare that everything was all right. But he wasn't too worried. Dogs usually liked him, and the pan of food ought to make a good peace offering.

No sound came from the tool shed. Putting the pan on the ground, he took out the key and unlocked the padlock. Then he picked up the food, and holding it out in front of him, he slowly opened the door, while he said, "Good dog. Good dog, Nightmare," in a calm soothing voice. The shed was empty.

For just a moment he was seized by a weird dreamlike idea that something entirely supernatural had happened. That Nightmare hadn't been a real dog after all—that he'd somehow dematerialized or turned into something entirely different. Or that the whole thing had been an incredibly vivid dream, or some kind of crazy vision. But then he noticed the broken plank.

The toolshed, like all the buildings on the property, was very old, and the wood was possibly a little deteriorated, but still it must have taken a lot of force to tear the plank loose. On closer inspection, it was apparent that the loose plank, as well as the one next to it, had been scratched until they resembled some kind of wide-ribbed wooden corduroy—and until the nails holding them had pulled free from the flooring.

After he'd pushed the plank back more or less in place and pulled the lawn mower and a five-gallon gasoline can over in front of the scratched places, David went out and searched the yard. There was no sign of Nightmare anywhere.

Every one else was waking up when he got back in the house. As David tiptoed down the upstairs hall, Amanda popped out of her room, and a moment later Janie and Esther appeared. They all followed David into his room, where Blair was just climbing out of bed.

The little kids took the news calmly. "He'll come back tonight," Esther said, and Blair nodded. "He doesn't like to be shut up."

"But what if he doesn't?" Amanda said. "What if he goes back to wherever he came from?"

"He's come back a lot of times before," David reminded her.

"Yeah, but he might stop. Or something might happen to him. Like what if he meets those prisoners out there, and they shoot him or something. We've got to find a better way to keep him here."

David shook his head. "I don't think it's going to be easy."

"We could keep him in the house," Esther said.

Blair looked delighted. "He could sleep with me."

"Don't be ridiculous," David said.

"Who's being ridiculous now?" It was Molly, standing in the doorway. Everyone whirled around and stared at her, and then they all started talking at once.

"The Bleep was," Amanda said.

"Tesser was," Janie said.

"I was not," Esther said.

"Everybody shut up," David said. "Did you want something, Molly?"

Molly laughed. "Not me. I just wondered if anybody else did. Like breakfast, for instance."

It was Saturday. The longest Saturday in the history of

civilization. All day long David tried to get interested in things he usually looked forward to doing on weekends, with no luck at all. He wound up spending most of the day prowling restlessly around the house and yard, running into other members of the family who seemed to be prowling around, too. Where the kids were concerned, the reason was obvious, but they weren't the only ones. Jeff and Molly also seemed to be restless, and they didn't even know about Nightmare.

Right after lunch Pete showed up briefly. One of his older brothers had dropped him off to pick up the motorcycle, but he had to get right back to the farm.

"I got work to do," he told David. "My old man said he'd have my hide if I didn't come right back." He leaned forward suddenly and David stiffened, but Pete only whispered hoarsely. "How's the mutt?"

When David explained, he shook his head. "Hey, that's too bad. But maybe the kid's right. Maybe he'll show up again."

David said he hoped so, and Pete nodded and then stood there for a while, astraddle the motorcycle, but not making any move to start it up. "How about Amanda?" he said at last.

David was puzzled. "What about Amanda?" he asked.

"What does she think—about the mutt?"

"She thinks he'll come back tonight, I guess," David said. "At least she hopes he will."

"Yeah. Well-uh-where is she?"

"Oh, she's around," David said quickly. "She was out here just a few minutes ago."

"Oh yeah? Well, I got to be going, I guess," Pete said,

but he didn't. At least not for several more minutes. He got off the motorcycle and started fiddling around with it—checking the oil and looking in the gas tank in between looking around the yard and up at the windows of the house. But at last he climbed on the bike and roared off down the road.

An hour or two later David was sitting on the back steps looking toward the hills and thinking, when Janie suddenly came out and banged the door behind her. Then she stomped across the porch and sat down beside him with her chin on her fists.

"What's the matter?" David asked.

Janie sighed. "I don't get any allowance tomorrow."

He tried to keep from grinning. Janie lost her allowance more often than any kid in the family, in spite of the fact that she really liked money a lot. "What've you been up to this time?"

"Nothing." Janie's voice squeaked with indignation. "But I said I was." Suddenly she raised her head. Her eyes lit up, and the frown wrinkles disappeared from her forehead. "It was a sacrifice. A noble sacrifice just like in *Hans Brinker and the Silver Skates*. I sacrificed my allowance for Nightmare."

"What are you talking about?" David said.

"Dad heard me talking to Blair about Nightmare."

"Janie!"

"It's all right. He didn't hear very much—just something about Blair talking dog language. But then he made me come in his study, and he scolded me about playing imaginary-dog with Blair. So I had to confess and say I was sorry and everything. And he said didn't I remember that I'd promised not to, and so I said yes, and then he said I don't get any allowance this week. But I didn't squeal."

So David congratulated her on her noble sacrifice and promised to give her part of his allowance. That really cheered her up a lot. After a while she said, "Could you tell Amanda and the twins about it? About how I had to sacrifice my allowance? And tell them to give me some of theirs, too. Okay?"

Then David said didn't she think her sacrifice would be a lot less noble that way, and she said she'd rather be unnoble than broke. So he agreed to ask Amanda and the twins, and Janie got up off the steps and skipped across the yard to the swing tree and started swinging.

It was just a little later that David heard Dad and Molly quarreling. He'd decided to do a little reading, and he was on his way to his room to get a book when he heard voices coming out of Dad's study.

"Lots of children have imaginary friends when they're little," Molly was saying, "and I don't think it hurts them a bit. I think it's an indication of a rich inner life."

"I agree." Dad was using the super calm voice he used when he was arguing. "Lots of children of three or four. But Blair is six. And Mrs. Bowen sees it as part of a larger pattern —a pattern of failure to deal with reality. Of his lack of ability to hear and follow instructions, for instance."

"That woman!" Molly's voice was angry. "If I were Blair's teacher, I'd make a big thing about Blair's dog. I'd help him write stories about it, and I'd have the whole class draw pictures of it."

"But you're not his teacher," Dad said.

"I know, but I am his mother—all right, stepmother—but I feel like his mother. And I'm not going to stop him if he wants to tell me about his dog. Not even if you take away my allowance, too, like poor little Janie."

David didn't want to listen. It was a lot like the way you crane your neck to stare at accidents on the highway, knowing you'll hate it if you see anything and yet not able to stop. So he went on listening, and hating it, until he heard someone on the stairs. Then he hurried on to his own room.

On the window seat with a good book, he couldn't keep his mind on what he was reading. Even though he kept reminding himself that Dad and Molly got along great most of the time, and that a little argument now and then didn't necessarily mean divorce or any thing like that, he couldn't seem to relax and forget about what he'd overheard. It was as if the quarrel about Blair's dog kept getting mixed up with other more distant memories—memories of losing one mother already, and the fact that Molly had already gotten one divorce.

He went on sitting there, staring at his book, until Blair came in and got Rolor out of his cage and started playing with him on the floor. Blair was trying to teach the crow how to play checkers. So far Rolor had learned to wait for his turn and then to hop over and pick up a red checker. What he did with the checker didn't usually make a whole lot of sense, but still it was a pretty good start—for a crow. On about his fourth move he actually jumped one of Blair's checkers, and David got really excited; but after that things started going downhill. On his next turn Rolor flew back to his cage with the checker and put it in his water dish. The whole scene wasn't too enlightening, but it was a lot more entertaining than reading the same paragraph over six times and worrying.

It wasn't exactly what you would call relaxed at dinner that night. In fact, if the dinner table and everyone around it had been balanced on a high wire over the Grand Canyon, there couldn't have been more careful consideration of every move. It figured. The kids were all keyed up about Nightmare—worrying if he would be back tonight as well as worrying that somebody was going to get careless and give away the whole secret. And it was pretty obvious that Dad and Molly were hiding something, too.

Actually they were smiling a lot and being super polite and thoughtful to each other—answering very quickly when the other one spoke and passing each other things they already had a plate full of. If you didn't know, you might think they were a couple of very nice people—who just happened to make everyone around them want to scream. But of course David knew. They hadn't finished quarrelling yet.

As usual, Blair went to sleep almost immediately after dinner. Watching him conking out right in the middle of a story Molly was reading to him and Esther, David remembered wondering why Blair's tendency to sleep a lot seemed to be getting worse. He'd worried about it, and he knew Molly and Dad had, too. It was too bad they couldn't be told that there was a perfectly logical reason for it. It was too bad he couldn't say, "It's nothing to worry about, Molly. It's just that he spends a couple of hours every night playing with his dog." That would really fix things up. Or—he suppressed a grin—he might say, "It's just that he has a Nightmare that wakes him up every night."

Bedtime came at last, but David didn't sleep. Or at least he didn't plan to. But he was doing something very like it when he heard Blair calling him. He immediately leaped out of bed and staggered to the widow where Blair was looking out into a still dark night.

"He's there," Blair said. "Nightmare's down there. I'll go tell Janie and Tesser." A few minutes later they were all out in the garden gathered around Nightmare as he wolfed down a big panful of food.

He didn't growl at all that night. He sniffed at each of them in turn before he started eating; and when he finished, he went around again sniffing and licking their hands as if he were saying thanks. The little kids all patted him, so when he came to David, he tried it too; and the dog didn't seem to mind. Pretty soon they were all patting him at once.

It was a strange sensation, patting a dog whose head was almost as high as your chin. There was a heavy choke collar on the strong, thick neck, but no license or identification tags. The rough shaggy coat felt softer than it looked, but under the hair the bones were very close to the surface. Each knob on the backbone was clear and distinct, as were the huge arching bones of the ribcage. It seemed that, in spite of all the food scrounging Janie and the twins had been doing, Nightmare hadn't really been getting enough to eat.

"Poor old boy," David said. "Poor dog." And Nightmare did something mournful-looking with his shaggy eyebrows and drooped his ears flat against his head. He looked so sorry for himself that they all laughed, and he liked that. He bounced around bumping into people and licking their faces —and when a dog as tall as Nightmare wanted to lick your face, there wasn't much you could do about it, except let him.

David was scratching the side of Nightmare's head just above his eye when his fingers hit a lump. Under the shaggy hair was a long rough welt that ran for several inches along the side of the huge head. "Hey, Blair," David said. "What's this?"

"Somebody hurt him," Blair said. "It's almost well now."

Amanda and David examined the almost healed wound and then stared at each other. "Somebody shot him," Amanda whispered.

David nodded.

Chapter Twelve

Someone had shot Nightmare and almost killed him. David felt a rush of anger, and then a fierce determination to keep it from happening again. To somehow find a way to keep Nightmare from wandering around where somebody might take another shot at him.

"I bet those prisoners shot him," Janie said.

For once one of Janie's theories made some sense. The prisoners supposedly had a gun, and they were out there somewhere in the same area where Nightmare had been living. "Could be," David said.

"I'll bet it was that troll, Golanski," Amanda said.

"No, Golanski has a shotgun," David reminded her. "This wasn't done by bird shot. It was a big bullet."

"Well, I bet somebody shot him when he was prowling around trying to find food in their yard. We just have to find some way to keep him here—in our own yard."

Which was exactly what David had been thinking. The question was how. Where could they put him where he'd be safe and where Dad and Molly wouldn't find him? There were a couple of other old outbuildings on the Stanley property, but only the tool shed was isolated enough to be fairly safe, and they'd already found out how Nightmare felt about being shut up in the tool shed. There would have to be some other way.

They stood in a circle with Nightmare in the center for a long time, arguing about how to keep him from wandering around at night and getting shot at. For a while he sat there, looking from one to the other as they talked, as if he were listening carefully to their suggestions. But finally he gave a big sigh and collapsed with his head on his paws. They all laughed. It seemed funny somehow for such a huge animal to act so much like a normal dog.

There didn't seem to be any possible solution. Even if they could find a place to shut him up at night, he would probably have to be released during the day when they were all away at school. It was beginning to seem hopeless. The suggestions got more and more ridiculous, and meanwhile, the temperature in the garden seemed to get colder and colder. At last they decided they would just have to go on doing exactly what Blair had been doing—feed Nightmare every night and then let him go back to wherever he went—and hope for the best.

"Maybe if we buy some real dog food and feed him all he can possibly eat, he'll at least stay out of other people's yards and spring houses," David said through chattering teeth. "Come on, kids. We'd better go in. There's nothing more we can do tonight." He gave Nightmare one last pat and told him good-by. "I guess you're on your own until tomorrow, big boy. Same time, same place." It wasn't good enough, but there didn't seem to be any other solution. One at a time the others hugged or patted Nightmare, and slowly and reluctantly, they all started for the back door. Nightmare trotted along behind.

"I guess he remembers coming in last night," Amanda said. "He'll go away as soon as we all go in." That was all she knew about it. As soon as they all went in, Nightmare started to whine. They all stopped in their tracks and stared at each other in horror, and then up toward where Dad and Molly were sleeping—or at least, had been sleeping. Silence. No sound from Nightmare and none from upstairs, either. David was just breathing a sigh of relief when there was a loud scratching noise. Just one long scratch, but it sounded like one more and there wouldn't be any door left. David jerked the door open, and Nightmare bounced into the kitchen like a playful puppy. Like about one hundred and fifty pounds of playful puppy.

He wound up sleeping on Blair's bed. It was crazy. All night long David told himself it was crazy. What if Molly came in to see if Blair was sleeping all right. She didn't do it very often, but this could be the night she decided to. And what was going to happen in the morning. It was the kind of thing he hated to think about in the middle of the night.

But in spite of the craziness of it all, there were times that he felt really good about it: two or three times in fact, when he reached over and turned on his bed lamp just to check to see if everything was all right—and there he was flaked out across most of Blair's bed like some kind of enormous stuffed toy. When the light went on, Blair just went on sleeping peacefully, but each time Nightmare lifted his head and kind of grinned at David and thumped his ridiculously long tail on the bedspread.

David didn't sleep very much, but toward morning he was snoozing when the alarm went off. He sat up with a start. Blair's bed was empty. No Nightmare and no Blair either. David leaped to his feet and rushed out into the hall. He was down the stairs and through the hall and into the kitchen before he was fully awake. The door was open, and Blair was standing on the steps looking out toward the back yard and the hills behind. David staggered out onto the porch.

"Blair," his voice was still sleep-logged and creaky. "What happened? Where is he?"

"Hi, David," Blair said. "He woke me up, so I brought him downstairs, and he went away. I told him not to come back until it's dark."

Early that afternoon they decided to hold a council of war in the tree house. It was a little bit crowded, but it seemed like the safest place. They could see anyone coming from a long way off, so they didn't have to worry about eavesdroppers. And in case Dad or Molly got curious and came snooping around, they were all prepared to start hammering and sawing at a moment's notice. They'd barely gotten started, however, when from out near the garage a familiar voice yelled, "Hey, Davey. Where are ya?"

"Ye gods," David said. He stuck his head out of the eight-sided window and yelled back, and Pete Garvey sauntered across the yard, grinning like a jack-o-lantern. By the time

Pete had crowded into the tree house, David's shoulder was jammed under a window ledge and his left leg had disappeared under three or four other people's. Under the circumstances, he sure hoped Dad didn't turn up and force them to put on their construction-crew act. One swing of the hammer now, and somebody was apt to get a concussion.

They stayed up in the tree house for about an hour, all six of them, and when it was over, they'd come up with what seemed like some very useful decisions. First of all, they decided to go on doing what Nightmare had forced them to do the night before. As soon as he'd had his dinner, they'd bring him upstairs and keep him there the rest of the night. That would take care of what was probably the most dangerous period for him to be wandering around the neighborhood. Also they would all take turns playing with him a little during the night—which would not only be fun but would also keep him awake so that he'd be more apt to spend his days quietly sleeping.

The other conclusion they came to was that they probably needed to feed him a lot more. For one thing, he was obviously skinnier than he ought to be, and if he was really well fed, he'd be a lot less apt to snoop around in places where he might get into trouble. That left only one problem. What to feed him. Janie offered to do some more research on Irish wolfhounds to find out what they ought to eat, but Pete seemed to think he already knew.

"Shoot," he said. "They're just like any mutt, only bigger. What he ought to have is kibble. That's what we feed our dogs."

"We got some for him once," Janie said. "Five whole pounds. But it didn't last very long."

"You ought to get the fifty pound bags at the feed store. It's a lot cheaper that way."

"Hey, yeah," David said. "We get King Tut's food there. Maybe we could tell Dad that King Tut needs some more grain and get him to drive us over there, today."

"Sure," Amanda said. "How're we going to bring a fifty-pound bag of kibble home in the car without him noticing?"

That one took a little figuring, but eventually they worked it out. By the time they'd left the tree house, everyone knew exactly what part to play in the dog food caper. All in all, it was a very profitable meeting. David climbed down the ladder feeling really great, in spite of a stiff neck and a nearly petrified left leg.

After hiding what was left of King Tut's turkey food and making the other necessary preparations, David approached Dad with the suggestion that they ought to go to the feed store, and it worked like a charm. Dad said he had to run into town to go to the hardware store, and they might as well go right away. He did seem a little surprised when it turned out that the whole family, including Pete Garvey, wanted to go along. But he didn't say anything. And if he noticed that they were all rather peculiarly dressed for an unusually warm November day, he didn't say anything about that either. David checked all the kids to make sure they had remembered their financial contributions and the other things they were going to need, and then they all piled into Dad's station wagon.

On the way there Amanda quietly collected everyone's money. They all coughed up what they'd promised, even Janie. Looking mournful but determined, she slowly handed over most of what she'd gotten by making a big deal out of her "noble sacrifice." Even Pete fished around in his pocket and dropped a few coins into Amanda's hand. When they got to the feed store, they all scattered out and got ready to put the rest of the plan into effect.

David's first job was to pick out something interesting that the little kids could talk Dad into looking at—and fortunately there were baby mallards in the brooder. As soon as the turkey grain was purchased, Janie and the twins went into their act, insisting that Dad come look at the ducklings—so that Amanda could buy the kibble without his noticing. The next part was where Pete really came in handy. Pete's assignment was to carry the fifty pound bag to the men's restroom where David met him.

Afterwards it occurred to David that he'd taken an awful chance. Not only had he been alone with Pete in the restroom, but he'd actually handed him his pocketknife. Talk about stupid moves. But he lucked out. Apparently Garvey was so caught up in the kibble scheme that he didn't even notice he was missing a wonderful opportunity. All he did was slit open the kibble bag—Amanda had decided on Tender Chunks—and start filling pillowcases, which David proceeded to fasten shut with safety pins. Even though Pete was bigger, he wasn't able to wear as much kibble as David, because he only had a windbreaker to hide it under and David had worn his bulgy down jacket. After they'd filled a big bag for David and a middle-sized one for Pete, they fixed up a small one for Blair, who was supposed to have slipped away from the ducklings by then and joined them in the restroom. Only he hadn't.

They were still waiting, on pins and needles, when Amanda banged on the door and yelled, "Hurry up in there." The minute they opened the door, she grabbed the kibble bag and, dragging it behind her, she rushed down the hall to the ladies' restroom.

Holding his own pillowcase against his chest under his jacket and carrying Blair's, David hurried after her and caught up just as she got to the door to the ladies' room. "Here's Blair's," he said, handing her the small pillowcase. "He didn't show up."

"Go get him," she hissed. "Go get all of them."

In the brooder room, Dad and the three little kids were still enthusiastically admiring the ducklings. Clutching his Tender Chunks, David joined them. "Hi, Dad," he said. "Sorry to keep you waiting. I was in the restroom. In the RESTROOM," he repeated, glaring at the kids.

"Oh!" Janie jumped as if she been shot. "I have to go to the RESTROOM."

"Me too," Esther said. "YOU TOO, BLAIR."

"Oooh," Blair said, looking at Dad. "I have to go to the restroom.

"Well, go then, but hurry." He smiled at David. "Must be an epidemic."

"I guess so. I'll go hurry Blair up."

Dad looked puzzled, but he didn't argue. "I'll be in the car," was all he said. "Waiting."

David caught up with Blair as he was about to go into

the men's room, grabbed him by the arm and pulled him down the hall. Outside the ladies' room he could hear a lot of frantic whispers coming through the thin door. "Here's Blair," he yelled. The door opened, and Amanda's arm came out and grabbed Blair by the front of his jacket. Blair held onto David's arm with both hands.

"I can't go in there," he said.

"You have to," David said grimly. "That's where the kibble is." He pulled his arm free, and Blair disappeared into the ladies' room.

A few minutes later when they all filed out of the feed store clutching their chests, Dad was sitting impatiently behind the wheel. As they climbed carefully into the station wagon, he said, "I suppose I have only myself to blame for not reminding you before we left home."

Amanda rolled her eyes at David. She was biting her lip and making sizzling noises like smothered explosions. David looked away quickly. By staring out the window he managed to keep a straight face until Dad pulled up at the hardware store and got out. The minute the door closed behind him, Amanda began to giggle and pretty soon they were all roaring with laughter—even Pete. It took him longer to get started, but once he did, he laughed harder and certainly louder than any of them. They went on laughing until they saw Dad coming back.

When they got home, Dad parked the car in the garage, and after he'd gone into the house, the rest was easy. They emptied their pillowcases into a big box and hid it under the workbench. They were ready for Nightmare's next visit.

Pete said he had to go home then, and when they

thanked him he shrugged and said it "wasn't nothing" and he wished he could stay to help some more. "I wish you could, too," David said, but he didn't mean it. He was grateful for the help, of course, but he still had a very strong feeling that Pete's reason for hanging around wasn't just an urge to be neighborly. Yet, somehow he felt there wasn't any great need for him to go on biking to school. And that was a big relief.

That night Nightmare ate a huge amount of kibble and then slept until early morning on Blair's bed, just as he had before. But this time David didn't have to turn on the light to remind himself that it was all really true. All he had to do was sniff his pillowcase. It smelled exactly like Tender Chunks.

Chapter
Thirteen

When Janie said she was going to do some more research about Irish wolfhounds, David had said, "Sure, go ahead" without thinking much about what she might come up with. If he expected anything, it was just some information about the origin of the breed and maybe something about their care and feeding. But the actual results of her research reminded him (not that he needed reminding) that you shouldn't underestimate the power of a woman. Particularly not an eight-year-old one named Jane Victoria Stanley.

When David and Amanda got home on Monday, the three little kids were waiting on the front porch. The minute they saw the bus, they jumped up and ran to meet it. At first they all three talked at once—even Blair—and it was impossible to understand what any of them were saying.

"Hey, cool it. Cool it," David said several times before he got any results. "One at a time. Okay?"

"Okay. Me. I'm the one." Janie said. "I was the one who found out, so I get to tell them. Shut up, Tesser."

"Tell us what, wimp?" Amanda said.

"I found out about Nightmare. I found out all about where he came from and why he's afraid of people and who shot him and everything."

"Ye gods," David said, and then nobody said anything for a long time, except for Janie—and what she said was really amazing. Leave it to Janie.

It seemed that Janie's research had included telling everyone in her class that she was going to write a report on Irish wolfhounds and that she needed to interview people who owned one or knew something about them. And right away a girl in her class said she knew a girl in the fifth grade whose uncle used to own one. So then Janie talked to the fifth grade girl, whose name was Corinne Plenty, and that's when she got the whole story.

As soon as Janie asked her about her uncle's dog, this Corinne started telling about how her uncle—whose name was Sam Plenty and who was a real creep—bought an Irish wolfhound for a watch dog about a year ago. Corinne couldn't remember exactly when. He owned a big car wrecking business in Riverport, called Plenty's Auto Parts. He bought expensive foreign cars that had been in accidents and sold parts off them. But he'd been having a lot of trouble with kids who climbed the fence around his wrecking yard at night and stole car parts, so he decided to get a watch dog.

According to Corinne her uncle was so furious about losing all his car parts, he decided to buy a young dog and raise it to be a mankiller. He wanted it to be very big and dangerous, so when he heard that Irish wolfhounds were the biggest breed, he decided that that was what he was going to get. So he went to an Irish wolfhound kennel, and even though the people there told him they were gentle, good-natured dogs, he bought one anyway. He told Corinne's mother that it wouldn't be good-natured when he got through with it. The first thing he did was send it to a special school to have it attack trained. When it came back from the training school, it knew all its attack commands, but it was still a friendly, gentle dog. So then the uncle began his own training program.

"Corinne said Jaws—that's what her uncle called the puppy—Jaws was a real sweet dog at first, but that her uncle beat it all the time to make it mean and shut it up in a tiny dark room all day so it would learn to sleep in the daytime and stay awake at night to keep people out of the junk yard." Janie stopped and looked from David to Amanda and back again.

"Ye gods," David said.

"After a while it started to get mean and afraid of people, particularly men. And then, just when Corinne's mother was about to report her own brother-in-law to the S.P.C.A., they found out it was too late. Jaws was dead."

"Dead?" David and Amanda said together.

"That's what she said," Janie said. "She said that one day they went to visit the uncle and he had this big bandage on his arm. When they asked about it, he said Jaws had bitten him and he'd had to have twenty-seven stitches. So then they said where was Jaws, and he said 'He's dead. I took the blankety-blank-blank out in the woods and shot him.' "

"What woods?" Amanda asked.

"She didn't know," Janie said. "I asked her, but she didn't know. But her uncle lives in Riverport, and there's no woods right around there."

"And if he drove up the freeway the closest woods would be right around here," David said.

"But he was a lousy shot." Amanda was looking very excited. David couldn't remember ever seeing her look so excited, except maybe when they'd been kidnapped in Italy. "And the bullet must have just creased Nightmare's head and stunned him, so the jerk thought he was dead and went off and left him. That is the most totally gross thing I've ever heard in my whole life. I hope he got blood poisoning and rotted. It's a wonder it didn't poison Nightmare, biting a rotten person like that."

"No wonder he doesn't like to be shut up in small places," David said.

"Yeah, and no wonder he's so much more suspicious of Pete than he is of the rest of us. I mean, if he hates men." Amanda shrugged. "Not that Pete is one, but he's as big as one."

David grinned. "Smart dog," he said under his breath.

"See," Janie interrupted. "Aren't I a great detective?"

This time, they all had to agree that she was.

There didn't seem to be much doubt that Blair's Nightmare and Sam Plenty's Jaws were one and the same, but still David waited impatiently for the nightly visit—and a chance to check out some of Janie's information. That night, instead of depending on Blair's mysterious inner alarm, he turned his own ordinary alarm clock to soft, and set it for eleven o'clock. Blair was still asleep when it went off. David started getting dressed—down jacket, pants, heavy socks and sneakers —he'd learned his lesson about November midnights—when the door opened noiselessly and Amanda came in, followed closely by Janie and Esther. A few minutes later Blair sat up in bed, suddenly and amazingly wide-eyed and alert.

They went downstairs then, a silent single file, tiptoeing carefully down the hall past Dad and Molly's door and then downstairs and into the kitchen. Janie got out some leftovers from where she'd stashed them at the back of the broom closet, while David went to the garage for kibble, and in a few minutes they were in the garden.

It was a foggy night and the heavy white mist blurred the beam of their flashlights, reflecting the light backwards to dazzle their eyes. At first the garden seemed empty. David turned slowly in a circle, shining his light into the misty darkness under the shrubs and bushes.

"There he comes," Blair whispered, just as a shapeless shadow, caught in the beam of the flashlight, darkened and thickened, and transformed itself into a monstrous form. David gasped—he still wasn't used to the size of Nightmare. A second later he was saying hello, beating them with his wagging tail and licking their faces.

He was almost through eating when Amanda nudged David. "You try it," she said. "I guess you'd sound most like a man."

David backed off a few steps and then, in a deep voice, said, "Jaws! Here Jaws!"

Nightmare's head jerked up and he spun around, tail tucked and lips lifted in a snarl.

"Good dog, Nightmare," David said quickly.

Tail wagging sheepishly, Nightmare bounced over to him and licked his face, as if apologizing for making an embarrassing mistake. Some of the others tried calling him Jaws, but after that first time he stopped reacting so violently. Instead he hung his head and looked mournful, as if they'd said "no" or "bad dog." There was no doubt about it—the word Jaws meant something to Nightmare.

Although what Janie had found out solved a lot of the mystery about where Nightmare came from and why he did some of the things he did, it didn't solve any of the problems. As a matter of fact, in some ways, it only gave them more things to worry about. Like, what might happen if Nightmare were discovered. If Dad insisted on turning him over to the pound, he would probably be traced to his former owner—who could either decide that he wanted him back or that he was vicious and demand that he be killed.

And there was another problem that occurred to David. What might happen to Dad if he suddenly came face to face with Nightmare? Dad was obviously a man, and a pretty big one, too. Nightmare couldn't be expected to know that he was not like Sam Plenty. David thought about that possibility when, with Nightmare padding along beside him, he crept back up the stairs—and down the hall right past Dad and Molly's door. When he and Blair and Nightmare finally got to their room and closed the door behind them, David found himself gasping for air—and realized that he hadn't been doing much breathing for quite a long while.

As soon as they got in the room, David locked the door. He hadn't locked it before because he realized that if Dad or Molly came to the door while Nightmare was in the room it was all over anyway. They would, of course, want to come in and find out why the door was locked, and that would be that. Having the door locked wouldn't make it any safer for Nightmare. However, David now realized, it might very well make it a whole lot safer for Dad or Molly—particularly Dad. At least with the door locked there would be time to warn Dad to come in slowly and quietly and to explain to Nightmare that Jeffrey Stanley was "good" and a very different kind of man from Sam Plenty.

David explained it all to Blair, and it was clear that he understood and agreed that it was the only thing to do. So David started locking the bedroom door at night—and it was only a couple of nights later that it happened, just as he'd been afraid it would.

That night there'd only been three of them down to feed Nightmare and play with him and bring him upstairs to sleep. Amanda had told David ahead of time not to wake her up. When he had gone upstairs to bed, she said she still had a lot of homework to do, and she was going to get to bed late, and she'd need all the sleep she could get. And then Tesser had decided it was too cold and chickened out, too. So it was only Janie and Blair and David who went down and mixed up the kibble and leftovers and took them out to Nightmare in the garden.

It was a nice clear night with an almost full moon, and when Nightmare finished eating, they all went out behind the garage and played tug-of-war with an old pair of Dad's jeans. Nightmare loved to play tug-of-war. However, with only three people on the other side, it wasn't really much of a contest. David took hold of one pants leg and Janie and Blair took hold of David, and then Nightmare took the other pants leg in his teeth and pulled them all over the backyard. When they were all worn out, he didn't want to quit. Nightmare really liked winning.

He was still feeling especially playful when they started into the house, and David had to tell him to be quiet and stop bouncing around. That is, David told Blair to tell him, since he minded Blair a lot better than anyone else. But halfway up the stairs, he started frisking again and bumped into David and made him stumble. It didn't seem to David that they'd made very much noise at all, and he was just congratulating himself on a narrow escape when something else happened. They'd made it safely to their room and David was just closing the door when Rolor let out a horrified croak. David had forgotten to cover the crow's cage, and Rolor had just set eyes on Nightmare for the first time.

David made a dive for the cage cover. He just had time for one glimpse of Rolor's bug eyes and bristling feathers before he blacked him out and shut him up. If it hadn't been so dangerous, it would have been funny. If crows have nightmares, Rolor must have thought he was having one.

While Blair climbed unconcernedly into bed and Nightmare stretched out beside him, David waited and listened and worried. It was almost beginning to seem as if they'd lucked out again, when it happened. David had locked the door and turned out the light and he was just crawling into bed when the doorknob rattled and Molly's voice said, "Boys. What's going on? Open the door."

David froze. "Blair," he whispered. "Tell him it's okay. Tell him that Molly is okay." Sitting on the edge of the bed in the darkness, he listened to a rustling noise and Blair whispering. When he had waited as long as he dared, he got up and with his heart pounding like a jackhammer, he turned on the lights and turned the key in the lock. He tried to hold the door half open while he started explaining, but Molly pushed it back and came right in.

"David?" she said. "What's going on? I've been hearing the strangest noises." And then before he could answer she said, "Where's Blair?"

David whirled around. Nightmare was gone and so was Blair. For a moment David's mind felt disconnected, like a bicycle with a broken chain. The wheels were spinning but nothing was happening. "Blair?" a voice croaked, and for just a split second he didn't realize it was his own. Then Blair came out of the closet.

"Blair," Molly said. "What were you doing in there? Why were you in the closet?"

Blair's eyes looked huge and round as marbles. "I was hiding," he said.

Molly had a strange expression on her face. She sighed deeply and said, "Oh dear." Then she went to Blair and hugged him and led him back to his bed.

David stole a glance at the closet. The door was slightly open but not enough to see much.

"Look, sweetie," Molly said as she tucked Blair in. "You mustn't worry about those bad men. They probably aren't around here at all anymore, or they'd have found them by now. If you and David really feel better with the door locked, it's all right with me, but you shouldn't sleep in the closet. Promise me you'll stay in bed, now."

"Okay," Blair said. "I promise."

Molly turned out the light when she went out. David lay still, except for shaking a little. He couldn't believe that they'd made it—that Molly had come and gone without knowing what was in the closet. "Hey, Blair," he whispered. "How'd you get him to stay in the closet like that."

"I left the door open," Blair said. "He doesn't like it when you close the door. And I told him to stay. He knows about stay."

A minute later Blair whispered again, and a huge shadowy form padded out of the closet and climbed up on his bed.

Chapter Fourteen

Early in the morning, a day or two after the narrow escape with Molly, David woke up with Blair thumping him on the shoulder. Groaning, he rolled over and pushed Blair's hand away. It felt early. Too early. He opened one eye and, just as he suspected, it was barely beginning to get light.

"Knock it off, Blair. What's the matter?"

"He didn't come. Nightmare didn't come home last night." Blair whispered.

David sat up with a start. In the faint light of not quite dawn, Blair's face looked puckered and pale, and there were reddish blotches around his eyes, which meant that he'd been crying.

"Are you sure?" David asked. "Maybe he came and we just didn't wake up."

Blair shook his head. "No," he said in a quavery voice. "He didn't come."

"Well, look," David said. "Maybe he just wasn't hungry. We've been feeding him a lot lately. He'll probably be here tonight, just like always. Now go back to bed, and don't worry."

Blair did as he was told. At least he went back to bed and worried quietly. But now David was wide awake and worrying, too. He was afraid it was his fault. He hadn't set his alarm the night before, depending on Blair's interior one to let him know when Nightmare had arrived. Maybe this time it hadn't worked. Maybe Nightmare had arrived, and waited, and gone away hungry. He was still worrying when Janie came in, asking why she hadn't been awakened to help feed Nightmare. By breakfast time everybody—that is, all the kids —knew, and when the meal was half over Molly asked if anything was wrong. "You're all so quiet," she said. They all said everything was fine, but Molly didn't look convinced.

It was a long day at school. David had a hard time keeping his mind on his schoolwork. At lunchtime he was coming out of the cafeteria when he saw Pete and his friend Jerry Wilcox heading towards the gym. Without stopping to think about it, he hurried after them.

"Garvey," he said, when he caught up. "Could I talk to you a minute?"

"Sure," Pete said.

David moved off the path, and Pete followed—and Jerry, his eyes bugging with curiosity, came sidling after them. "Disappear, Wilcox," Pete said, and Wilcox disappeared. David told Pete about Nightmare not showing up.

Pete nodded, scratching his head. "How's The Bleep taking it?" he asked. Pete had been picking up Amanda's nicknames for everybody.

"Not too good," David said. "You know, crying and stuff."

Pete frowned. Pete's normal expressions were: 1. his famous dangerous grin, and 2. a real "nobody home" type blank stare. The frown was an interesting change. "Hey," he said, shaking his head. "Look. You tell The Bleep he's probably just kinda sick and sleeping it off somewheres. Dogs do that a lot. They get a belly ache or something like that, and they go eat some grass; then they go find themself some place to hole up until they're feeling better, and they come back, good as new. Tell The Bleep if he's not back by Saturday we'll all go looking for him. I can come over Saturday and help."

"You mean go up in the hills?" David asked.

"Yeah," Pete said uncertainly, but then he grinned. "Well, if we all went together it ought to be safe enough. I mean, six to two are pretty good odds. You all going to be home Saturday?"

"I think so."

"Amanda too?"

"Far as I know."

Pete nodded. "You tell The Bleep I'll be over. Okay?"

"Sure," David said.

David headed across the lawn to the art building, feeling a little better. It had been kind of a relief to talk to someone about it. It wasn't until quite a while afterwards that it suddenly occurred to him that he'd actually gone up to Pete Garvey on the school grounds and started a conversation. It was something he would never have dreamed of doing—not even before the gruesome morning when Mrs. Baldwin had jeopardized his entire future by making him class monitor. It was really a strange thing for him to have done, and if he hadn't been so busy worrying about Nightmare, he might have given it a lot more thought.

He slept poorly that night, and so did Blair. Several times, finding himself awake, he turned on the light and found that Blair was awake, too—sitting up in bed or just lying there with his eyes wide open. And once he was crouched on the windowsill, staring out into the night. When it began to get light, Blair started to cry. "Let's go look for him, David," he kept saying. "He needs us."

"We can't," David told him. "We have to go to school. And besides, Dad wouldn't let us go out in the hills. You know what he said about not going out there until they catch those guys. We can't do it, Blair. We'll just have to wait for Nightmare to come back. You know what Pete said. He'll come back when he's feeling better." He'd told Blair what Pete had said about dogs holing up when they got sick, but he hadn't mentioned the possibility of a Saturday search party because he was sure Dad wouldn't let them go. "He'll come back. I'm sure he will. Just remember what Pete said. About how dogs get sick sometimes and doctor themselves by eating grass and resting for a while. That's probably what it is. Nightmare will come back. Just wait and see." David tried to sound confident, but he wasn't really. And Blair knew it.

When Molly called them to come to breakfast, David took Blair into the bathroom and washed his face and told him he had to stop crying, and he did. But when they went downstairs his face was still pale and there were bright pink blotches around his eyes. David was afraid Molly would notice, and she did.

Molly was the only one in the kitchen when David and Blair came in; and as soon as she saw Blair, she took him by the shoulders and stared at his face. "Blair," she said, "what's the matter?" Blair shook his head and went on shaking it. Finally she picked him up and sat him on the sinkboard and took his face between her hands. "Tell me, sweetie," she said, and Blair burst out sobbing and said, "My dog. My dog is gone."

"Oh Blair," Molly said. "Oh honey." And she picked him up off the sinkboard and carried him out of the room. The scrambled eggs were about to burn, so David went over and turned off the fire and scraped them out into a bowl. He felt strangely numb, or at least not any more worried than he had been before. He didn't think it mattered too much what Blair told Molly. She'd just suppose it was all his imagination; and besides, Nightmare was gone anyway. Dad couldn't very well send a missing dog to the pound.

When Molly and Blair came back, everyone was in the kitchen. Nobody said anything. It was another strange meal with lots of staring and not much conversation. David finished as quickly as he could and went upstairs to get his books. He was still in his room a few minutes later when Blair came in.

"I'm sorry," he said.

"What for?" David asked.

"For talking about Nightmare. To Molly. I forgot. I'm sorry, David."

"Look, Blair. Don't worry about it. It doesn't matter. She probably didn't believe you anyway. That Nightmare is a real dog, I mean."

Blair nodded. "She didn't," he said. "But she got mad. It made her very mad."

"Mad? At you?"

"Nooo," Blair said thoughtfully. "Not mad at me. But she's very mad at somebody."

"Ye gods!" David said. Then he looked at his watch and said it again. "Ye gods. I'm going to miss the bus."

He grabbed his books and ran. He was just turning the corner at the foot of the stairs when he heard voices coming from the direction of the living room.

He didn't hear much—there wasn't time to—but it was enough to give him a pretty good idea of what was going on and what the conversation was all about. If you could call it a conversation. Argument would be more like it—or quarrel—or even fight. At least that's what he would have called it, if it had been Janie and Esther yelling at each other like that—instead of Dad and Molly.

Amanda was already at the bus stop. She looked at David and looked away, and then looked back again.

"What's the matter?" she said.

David shrugged, staring at the ground.

"Tell me."

He shook his head.

"You want to get slugged?"

David looked up, quickly. "What for?" he said.

"For not telling me."

They stared at each other. Why not, he thought. Let her worry, too. "They're fighting again," he said. "Dad and Molly."

"Fighting?"

He nodded.

"What did they say?"

"Well, first—" he began, but just then the bus pulled to a stop. Amanda made him get on first, and when he started to sit down, she shoved him on down the aisle and kept shoving him until they got to the back of the bus. She let him sit down then and sat beside him.

"Go on," she said.

David looked up the aisle to where Amanda's friend, Tammy, and two or three other people had turned around and were staring back at them.

"Okay, Rabbit Ears," Amanda said. "This is a private argument, so butt out."

Tammy tossed her head and turned around, and after a second the rest of them did, too.

"Go on," Amanda said again.

"Well, Molly was kind of yelling and crying at the same time. She said something like, 'Can't you see what you're doing to him, Jeff. You and that Bowen woman. Making him kill his dreams. Trying to force him into some stupid pattern.' And Dad said something like, 'Calm down, Molly. I haven't forced him.' And she said, 'Yes, you have. You told him to get rid of his dreams, and he's done it and it's breaking his heart.' And Dad said, 'Oh Molly, stop being so dramatic.' And then she called him a computer-brained academic, and he called her a Celtic Niobe or something like that, and then I left."

"So?" Amanda said.

"So?" David stared at her, but then he got the picture. She just didn't care. In fact she'd probably be delighted if Dad and Molly decided to get a divorce. It was probably what she'd been hoping for all along. "Yeah," he said. "Well, I guess you'll be glad when they get a divorce."

"What?" She stared at him, and then after a moment she began to grin. "Divorce? Mom and Jeff? They're crazy about each other. What makes you think they're going to get a divorce?"

"Well, they've been fighting a lot lately."

"Fighting? You call that fighting? If you think that's fighting you should have seen her with my dad. That was fighting."

"Yeah?" Maybe Amanda was right. Maybe it wasn't as serious as it had sounded. "I don't know. My mom never fought with him like that."

Amanda shrugged. "So I've heard. But let me tell you— that wasn't normal. Most married people fight a lot, even the ones that are crazy about each other. Your mother must have been some kind of saint, or something. My mom is Irish, and I'll bet even the saints fight in Ireland."

David laughed.

"What are you laughing about?"

"I don't know. I just flashed on this bunch of saints bashing each other with their halos."

They both laughed. When Amanda stopped laughing,

she started frowning. "And what do you mean, I wouldn't care if they got a divorce?"

"Well, like, you told me lots of times how you felt about it—about getting a stepdad and a bunch of brothers and sisters."

She frowned harder. "When did I tell you that?"

"Well, a couple of years ago, I guess."

"Right." Amanda nodded. "A couple of years ago. A long time ago." She was frowning so hard that it was really making him feel antsy. He started to scoot away from her, but she grabbed his jacket and jerked him back. "What do you think I punched Garvey for?" she asked suddenly.

David's whole insides cringed. He looked up the aisle but no one was paying any attention. "Yeah," he said. "Because you felt sorry for the poor little chicken." He tried to say it coolly, but he could feel a very uncool rush in his face and neck.

Amanda glared at him. "You idiot. I didn't feel sorry for you. What I felt—all of a sudden—was 'you can't treat my brother that way.'" She looked away then, and when she looked back she was smiling the way she did when she was making fun of somebody, only this time it seemed to be herself. "Can you believe it? My brother! It really jolted me. You know what I mean?"

David nodded slowly. "Yeah," he said. It jolted him, too.

Chapter
Fifteen

"David the Daydreamer," Mrs. Baldwin called him that morning after the second time he goofed up when she asked him a question. And a couple of guys on his team called him much worse things during P.E. He couldn't help it. He really tried to keep his mind on what he was supposed to be doing, but it wasn't easy. Questions kept popping up and refusing to go away. Questions about Nightmare and Blair—and Amanda, too. It wasn't until school was over that he was free to relax and deal with the questions—and their possible answers.

The bus was late that afternoon, and it was very quiet at the bus stop. Pete had stayed after school for football practice, and Amanda had gone home with Eloise. So David finally had time to think about Nightmare—and poor old Blair—and what Amanda had said that morning—and about what was going to happen next. He had a very strong premonition that it was going to be something out of the ordinary. Even more out of the ordinary, that is, than what had been happening.

Later, on the bus, and particularly after it turned onto Westerly Road, the premonition became stronger, and sure enough, he'd just started down the driveway when Esther came running to meet him. "David," she said and started to cry.

"What's the matter?" he asked, but she only pointed toward the backyard and sobbed. A weird sort of chill that started somewhere in his throat began to crawl up David's neck and across his scalp. He took Esther by the shoulders and shook her hard. "Stop it," he said. "Stop it, Tesser. What is it?"

Esther choked, hiccupped, caught her breath, and started to talk. "Blair. It's Blair. He went to look for Nightmare—all by himself. I told him not to. I told him those bad guys would get him. But he went anyway."

"Ye gods," David said. He started to run toward the creek and the hills beyond, but after two or three steps he turned around and ran back.

"Where's Dad?" he asked Tesser.

"He's not home yet. And Molly went to get Janie at the dentist. She said you'd be home in a minute, but you weren't. And Blair wouldn't stay in the house like she told us."

"Okay," David said. "I'm going after him. He can't have gone very far. But if Molly gets back before we do, just tell her—just tell her you don't know where we are. I'll think up something when we get back. And stop crying. I'll find Blair. I promise."

"You promise?" Esther stopped crying. She smiled at David with big fat tears still running down her cheeks. "Okay. Okay. What am I supposed to tell Molly?"

"That you don't know where we are. Now go in the house and stay there until somebody gets home. Okay?"

"Okay," Esther said.

For the first five or ten minutes he ran hard. Somewhere along the way he noticed something thumping on his back and realized he was still wearing his backpack. As he ran he wondered how much of a head start Blair had. He hadn't thought to ask Esther, not that it would have made any difference. Time didn't mean anything to six year olds. But it couldn't have been very long. Molly wouldn't have gone off and left the twins alone unless it had been very close to the time for David to get home. He'd probably have made it in time to stop Blair if the bus hadn't been late.

He'd hoped to catch up with Blair before he got to the trees, but there was no sign of him on the long grassy slope that led up to the woods. David ran fast, without stopping at all on the open hillside, and only slowed a little when he got to the rougher ground of the creek bed. As he entered the woods, he began to call. Near heavy overhanging branches and heavy clumps of underbrush, where Blair—or anybody— might be standing unnoticed only a few feet away, he stopped, caught his breath and shouted. "Blair! Blair! Answer me. It's David." He listened for several seconds and then ran on. A few minutes later he stopped to call again.

By the time he'd crossed the small plateau between the two crests and then scrambled to the top of the higher second range, his legs were cramping and his lungs were aching so much he could barely call. He stopped for a moment at the top of the path that led down to the big valley and tried to catch his breath. His face burned and his throat ached and deeper down his whole insides were churning with fear for Blair—and with anger at him, too, for running off and causing so much trouble.

It didn't seem possible that Blair could have come so far. David wondered if he'd somehow passed him farther back—if there was any point in keeping on. He wondered if—and then he heard Blair calling. From somewhere down below on the heavily wooded slope a faint high-pitched voice called and stopped and called again. David plunged forward, running and sliding down the steep slope.

The calling went on, and in a few minutes David could make out the words. "Here, Nightmare," Blair was calling. "Here, Nightmare. Come. Come."

He caught up with Blair in a small clearing halfway down the hill. He was walking quickly toward the other side, but when he heard David coming he stopped and whirled around.

"David." Blair ran back toward him, looking happy and excited. David waited. It was so good to see him that he almost forgot how mad he'd been only a few moments before. "David. I heard him. He barked. Listen."

He turned around and, cupping his hands around his mouth, he called, "Nightmare," and a moment later David heard it too, distant but clear—a gruff deep-throated bark.

"Come on," Blair said and began to run. Forgetting all about the bawling out he was going to give Blair, David ran, too.

The clearing ended in a ravine with high, steep walls. David slid down to the bottom and then caught Blair as he half-jumped, half-fell down from the ledge above. Crossing the dry stream bed, David was looking for a way up the other side when Nightmare barked again. "That way," Blair said, pointing up the deep cleft in the hillside. "Up there."

The barking became steadily louder as they scrambled up the ravine, around boulders and over the trunks of fallen trees. They answered back, shouting, "Here we are, Nightmare. We're coming." At last the barking seemed to be all around them, echoing back from the steep cliffs on each side —and suddenly there he was, a huge, bristly, lop-eared face looking down at them from a ledge above the ravine.

A steep narrow path led up the cliff toward the ledge like a rough natural staircase with giant-sized risers. David scrambled up each step and then reached down to pull Blair up behind him. The last rise was a high one, and as David crawled up over it on his hands and knees, his forehead and eyes and nose received a bunch of enormous sloppy kisses. Then he was so busy hugging Nightmare and wiping off kisses and saying things like "Hi there, boy," and "Good dog," and "Cut it out," that he forgot all about Blair. But at last he remembered and pulled him up, and Nightmare went through the whole act again, kissing and nuzzling and just about knocking Blair off his feet with affection.

It was Blair who noticed the cut foot first. "Look," he said. "He's limping. He's bleeding, David. He's bleeding."

By then things had quieted down a little, and Nightmare was standing still—and holding his left front foot up off the ground. They made him lie down; and when they inspected the foot, they found a deep puffy-looking cut between the pads. When they turned his foot over to look at it, Nightmare looked too, sniffing and licking the cut, then looking up at them with a funny expression as if he were embarrassed, and apologizing for causing a fuss. Finally he put his chin down on the ground and lay still, only wagging his tail limply whenever they spoke to him or said his name. After a while he raised his head and sniffed at the pocket of Blair's jacket.

"Oh," Blair said, "I almost forgot." He dug in his pockets and brought out a few handfuls of kibble. Nightmare wolfed it down as if he were starving.

"See," Blair said. "I said he needed us. He's hungry. He's really hungry. And he's sick, David. I think he's sick."

"I don't think he's really sick," David said, "or he wouldn't want to eat at all. He's probably just weak from loss of blood. From the looks of things he really lost a lot of blood." He pointed to the rocky ground of the ledge. In several places there were big dark blotches of dried blood, and here and there there were a few fresh smears of bright red where he'd probably broken the wound open again in the excitement of greeting them. It was then, when David was looking at all the blood and thinking it was no wonder that Nightmare didn't feel very well, that he noticed something else.

Halfway hidden behind a jutting boulder, a long narrow crevice made a dark slash on the face of the cliff. It wasn't until David was moving toward it curiously, that he realized what it was—a cave. Inside the narrow entrance, the cave widened into a deep rocky cavern. He moved forward slowly, waiting for his eyes to adjust to the dim light.

"It's his house," Blair said. "It's Nightmare's house. It's where he goes everyday."

David turned around. Blair was standing in the entrance of the cave, and behind him was Nightmare. Limping badly, Nightmare moved ahead of them into the cave and then turned around and looked back and wagged his tail. David was thinking that he seemed to be welcoming them in, when Blair said, "He says come in. He wants us to come in."

There was a shallow depression in the soft mossy soil againt one wall and near it, half buried in the dust, a couple of large well-chewed bones. David picked one up and examined it, wondering if it might be the remains of Mr. Golanski's ham. He was still inspecting the bone when Blair said, "Look David. Is it real?"

It was real, all right, a pistol, heavy and dark and deadly-looking. Blair was holding it in both hands with the barrel pointing right toward David's legs. David took it away from him in a hurry. "Ye gods," he said under his breath.

Blair showed him where he'd found it, right there on the ground, half-buried under a bunch of dead leaves. It was dusty and there was dirt in the barrel, but there was no rust, and it didn't look all that old. David didn't know much about pistols, not even enough to know how you went about checking to see if they were loaded. He was examining it gingerly, making sure to keep the muzzle pointed at the ground, when Nightmare began to growl.

"No, Nightmare," Blair said. "It's all right," and the

growling stopped; but the dog's eyes were still on the gun and David could see that he was trembling. He kept watching, alert and tense, while David took off his backpack and put the gun in between his binder and his math book, and zipped it back up. It wasn't until the gun was out of sight that Nightmare wagged his tail sheepishly and limped over and licked David's hands, as if he were apologizing for distrusting him.

Even before Blair found the gun, David had been antsy to leave. The sun had disappeared over the western hills, and the sky was darkening. Under the trees it would soon be too dark to see the path. And—not too long ago someone had been to Nightmare's cave. Someone who carried a pistol. David had to make a decision in a hurry, and he decided that they had to take Nightmare with them. It was risky and it might be very hard to do, but there just wasn't any way they could go off and leave him—hungry and thirsty and with a wound that seemed to be festering.

"We'll take you home with us," Blair told Nightmare, which was exactly what David was thinking at the moment. "Won't we?"

"I guess we'll have to," David said.

"Right now?"

"Right now. As soon as we bandage his foot."

"What with?"

"My tee shirt," David said, taking off his jacket.

Fortunately the tee shirt was an old one and tore easily. David ripped it up, and after he'd wrapped the foot snugly, he tied the bandage in place with lots of long thin strips of shirt. Nightmare watched the whole proceeding with polite interest, and afterwards he didn't seem to limp quite as much when he walked. When David and Blair climbed down the path into the ravine, he followed slowly and carefully.

Nightmare stayed close beside them as they made their way down the ravine, but David noticed that he was breathing very hard, and if they stopped for even a moment he immediately lay down. He seemed weak and tired; but when they moved on, he struggled to his feet and followed. He followed, that is, until they reached the place where the path led up out of the ravine and on up to the top of the ridge. At that point Nightmare refused to follow. Instead he began to move on down the hill, walking more rapidly than he had before. When they called him, he looked back and whined and then went on.

"He wants us to come with him," Blair said and began to run. David followed, protesting, until he suddenly realized where they were going. The lake was only a few yards away, and Nightmare was probably very thirsty. David stopped arguing then and followed. He caught up with Blair and Nightmare just as they got to the lake.

At the edge of the lake David and Blair sat down and watched while Nightmare drank and drank for a long time, and then flopped down beside them panting, his long wet tongue lolling out one side of his mouth.

"He feels better now," Blair said.

David nodded. He felt better too—even though the water of the lake was already changing from blue to black and the long shadows under the trees were blurring into darkness. He was just opening his mouth to say they had better get going when Nightmare's head jerked up and he growled softly. Following the dog's gaze, David turned in time to see two men emerging from the underbrush only a few yards away.

Chapter Sixteen

The two men burst out from behind a clump of bushes and staggered a few steps toward the lake before one of them stopped. Leaning against the trunk of a tree, he slowly sank down to the ground. The other one went on a few steps before he stopped and went back. The one on the ground had a dirty gray blanket draped over his head and shoulders, but the other was wearing light blue denim pants and shirt, and there were some big white numbers on his back. For a moment he bent over the man in the blanket, and then he hurried on down to the lake. Stooping, he lifted some water in his cupped hands and was starting back—when Nightmare growled loudly. The man jerked as if he'd been shot and whirled around. David gasped, and then almost choked in horror. The man in blue denim had no face.

Until that moment David hadn't really been frightened.

Instead, when he realized what was happening, there was only a weird kind of sharpening of his senses, as if everything had suddenly gotten clearer and brighter. While the figures of the two men moving through the strange, colorless evening light seemed to be printing themselves on his brain, he was only feeling an excited curiosity—a kind of wonder about what was going to happen next. But then the man turned toward them.

Where the escaped prisoner's face should have been, there was only a shapeless discolored mass, with tiny slits for eyes. David swallowed hard. His heart was suddenly beating so hard it seemed about to explode. He jumped to his feet and reached for Blair. Nightmare was on his feet, too, and the hair on his back had risen into a stiff, bristly ridge. David took hold of his collar.

"Oh my God!" The faceless man staggered backwards until he bumped into the trunk of a tree. "Don't turn him loose," he said in a high-pitched whine. "Please, don't turn him loose." The other convict, the one on the ground, turned then, and there was a momentary glimpse of a thin, dark face with large sunken eyes. The eyes stared wildly, and the mouth opened and let out a strange high-pitched moan. He pulled the blanket up over his head and fell forward into a blanket-covered heap. The other man slid around behind the tree and peered out, and it was suddenly apparent that he wasn't actually faceless. It was just that his cheeks and forehead and even his nose were so blotched and bumpy and swollen that the whole hardly resembled a normal face.

"We give up," he said. "We're on our way to turn ourselves in. Hang on to that dog, kid. We give up. Honest."

David swallowed hard. His heart had stopped exploding, but his tongue felt stiff and uncooperative. He thought he ought to say something, but he couldn't think of anything that seemed appropriate. His first impulse was to say, "It's all right. The dog won't hurt you." But he quickly realized that might not be a good idea. Finally all he said was, "Who-o-o are you?" in a quavery voice, which was pretty stupid, because, of course, he knew who they were.

"Steve Hutter," the lumpy face said. "And that's Herbie Boston. He's real bad sick. I gotta get him to a hospital real quick."

"What's the matter with your face?" Blair said.

"My face?" The escaped prisoner named Steve Hutter moved cautiously out from behind the tree. "It's not just my face. It's all over me. Hang onto that dog, okay?" He pulled up the front of his shirt, and even in the dim light it was obvious that his stomach was just as red and lumpy as his face. "It's all over me. Poison oak. It's driving me crazy."

"Does he have poison oak, too?" Blair asked.

"Herbie? No. Not poison oak. He's got a lot worse than poison oak." Keeping his eyes on Nightmare, he took a step forward, glanced at the lump under the blanket, and put his hands up around his mouth. "He thinks he's got rabies," he whispered."

"Rabies?" David gasped. "Why does he think that? Did something bite him?"

Steve Hutter made a snorting noise. "Yeah, something bit him. That dog of yours almost bit his arm off, nine or ten days ago. His arm is swole up bigger'n a pumpkin, and he's burning up with fever."

"Nightmare bit him?" David said. Beside him, Nightmare was standing quietly but the hair was still up on his back, and now and then a soft growl rumbled in his chest. "Are you—sure?"

Hutter, who had begun to scratch frantically on both sides of his neck, stopped long enough to say, "Am I sure it was that dog that done it? Well, if it wasn't, it was one that looked just like him. You got some more big as that?"

"Well, look," David said. "Your friend couldn't have rabies if it was this dog that bit him—because Nightmare doesn't have rabies."

The man under the blanket swayed to a sitting position and pulled the blanket away from his face. His eyes looked wild and feverish. "Are you sure?" he asked in a croaking voice.

"I'm positive," David said. "If he bit you nine or ten days ago, and he was rabid then, he'd be dead by now. So he couldn't have had rabies when he bit you."

Herbie Boston, alias "The Weasel," stared at David with bloodshot sunken eyes and then threw back the blanket. "Look," he said.

But when David started forward, still hanging onto Blair with one hand and Nightmare with the other, The Weasel cringed away in terror.

"Keep away," he pleaded. "Keep him away from me."

So David told Nightmare to stay, and Blair to keep a tight hold on his collar, and then he moved a few cautious steps closer. Not too close though, in case the man under the blanket wasn't as sick as he was pretending to be.

The Weasel's right arm was in a makeshift sling made

from a strip of plastic that looked as if it might once have been a garbage bag. With his left hand he very carefully pushed the plastic back until David could see a swollen, discolored mass, punctured by a series of deep, festering indentations. It wasn't a pleasant sight.

Pulling the sling back in place, The Weasel cradled his arm against his chest and looked up at David with his strange feverish stare. Rabies or not, he was definitely sick—and frightened.

"It couldn't be rabies," David said, "but it might be blood poisoning. You'd better get to a doctor right away."

"Yeah," The Weasel said, "we got to get to a doctor."

Steve, the other convict, had edged out from behind the tree. "We was on our way to the road," he said. "We was going to flag down a car and ask them to call an ambulance—and the law. We was going to give ourselves up. Only Herbie couldn't go no farther."

David thought fast. The road was about half a mile away. In the other direction, Golanski's place was not much farther, and mostly down hill. And Mr. Golanski had a gun, in case the prisoners decided to change their minds about giving themselves up. "We could go to Mr. Golanski's," he said.

"Golanski's?" Steve said.

"The old coot with the shotgun," The Weasel muttered, rocking back and forth over his arm.

"I don't know," Steve said to David. "We thought about going there. But we been over that way before, and we seen that old guy with his cannon. He'd probably blow us away and ask questions afterwards."

"He wouldn't if we were with you," David said. "And it would be a lot easier to get there."

"The kid's got a point," The Weasel said.

They started out then with the two prisoners walking ahead—The Weasel with his good arm across the other guy's shoulders. David and Blair and Nightmare followed a few yards behind. They didn't dare get too close because every time they did Nightmare would growl and the two guys would start to panic. The whole procession moved very slowly, and then The Weasel collapsed and had to rest for a while before he could go on. Leaning against the trunk of a tree, he hugged his wounded arm and babbled about how sick he was and the terrible luck he'd had ever since he was born—how his mother died when he was six and his stepmother didn't like him, so he spent most of his time hanging out in the hills.

David believed him. At least he believed that he was sick. The feverish eyes and deliriously babbling voice were convincing. And the sad story about his childhood was probably true, too. David couldn't help feeling sorry for him. But at the same time, there was something about the slant of the thin mouth and the quick shifts of the dark eyes, that made him very glad Nightmare was on his side—his and Blair's.

"I grew up in these parts, kid," he said staring at David with his burning dark-rimmed eyes. "Used to swim in that lake back there when I was your age. Sometimes I used to hide out in the woods for a week at a time, snitching chickens and garden stuff from farms and cooking it over bonfires. Made out real well. Knew these woods like the back of my hand—what farms were easy pickin's and a lot of good hide-outs."

Steve stopped scratching his stomach and snorted. "Makes a good story, don't it?" His face was too messed up with poison oak to tell whether or not he was frowning, but he sounded angry. "Made it sound real good, Herbie did, about how we could hide out here for weeks, living off the fat of the land and hiding out in a cave that nobody'd find in a million years."

"A cave?" David asked.

"Yeah. Place he found when he was a kid. Only when we got there that hairy crocodile of yours had beat us to it, and when Herbie pulled his gun, he nearly got eaten alive. That was the end of the nice, safe cave-condo old Herbie promised me before we busted out." Steve stared at The Weasel bitterly. The Weasel ignored him and went on rocking his wounded arm. "End of our gun, too," Steve went on, starting to scratch again. "Couldn't get Herbie to go back with me to look for it. Told him I couldn't find it by myself. Me, I'm a city boy. Never saw a God d—" He looked at Blair, and then went on. "Never saw a tree 'cept in a park 'til I was a grown man. One mountain looks just like another to me."

For the first time since he'd put it away in his backpack, David remembered the gun. For a moment he considered getting it out—to make sure the convicts didn't change their minds about turning themselves in. But then he remembered he didn't even know if it were loaded, or if it had a safety catch on it, and how to get it off if it did. And then he flashed on a fact from a gun control debate in social studies—more homeowners who owned guns got shot than ones who didn't. If he got the gun out, it would be just his luck for the convicts to get it way from him. Besides, for the time being Nightmare seemed to be weapon enough.

David tuned back in on the conversation in time to hear Herbie, The Weasel, say, "Okay, so I'm scared of dogs. I can't help it. My stepmother used to threaten to sic her mangy old police dog on me, when I was a kid. I've had this thing about dogs ever since."

"Phobia?" David suggested.

"Yeah, that's right," The Weasel said to Steve. "I got me a phobia. What's your excuse? I didn't notice you rushing back into that cave after I dropped the gun."

"Well, hell," Steve said. "I thought we would go back later after the dog had gone off. I didn't know you wouldn't even go along to show me the way back."

"Look, man—" Herbie was starting when David interrupted.

"Hey, pardon me," he said. "But we'd better be going. It's just about dark. Do you think you could go on now—er— Mr. Boston?"

So The Weasel staggered to his feet, and they started off again towards Mr. Golanski's.

They were almost there, halfway across Golanski's cow pasture, when Blair tugged on David's arm pulling him to a stop.

"David," Blair said. "Mr. Golanski will tell—about Nightmare."

Blair was right. He should have thought of it himself. Suddenly David realized what he had to do. He yelled at the convicts to wait a minute and they did, leaning against the gate that led into the backyard.

David took off his backpack. Turning his back on Nightmare, he opened the pack and took out the gun, while he told Blair what to do. "You go on home with Nightmare," he said. "Take the shortcut through the orchard. And when you get home, put him in the tool shed. He'll probably stay there if you tell him to, and if you don't close the door. And if you get home before I do, just go on in and tell them I'll be along in a few minutes. Just as soon as I finish turning the escaped prisoners over to the police. Okay? You think you can find the way in the dark?"

"Nightmare knows the way," Blair said. "What's that for?"

"That's just in case they change their minds about turning themselves in when you take Nightmare away." David stuck the gun barrel under his belt and shrugged into his backpack. Then he waited until Blair and Nightmare had started back across the field.

The convicts were still leaning on the gate. When David called to them, they opened the gate and started across the yard. He took the gun out of his belt and held it in front of him with the barrel pointed down at the ground. It felt heavy and cold and deadly, and holding it made him feel very nervous. More nervous than he'd been since he first saw the prisoners by the lake.

It was very dark under the big trees in Golanski's yard. The convicts plodded along toward the lights of the house, without looking back. They didn't even seem to notice that Blair and Nightmare were no longer there. And David was pretty sure that they hadn't yet noticed the gun. He didn't intend to call their attention to it unless he had to.

The light was on in Mr. Golanski's kitchen. When they got to the house, David cleared his throat and said, "Knock on the door." His voice came out funny because of the nervousness, and instead of knocking Steve turned around and stared at him.

"Well, would you look at that," he said, and suddenly the whiney ingratiating tone was gone from his voice, replaced by a smooth, confident purr. "The kid's got a gun. Our gun from the looks of it. That kind of changes things, don't it, Weasel? I'll bet a sweet kid like that's not going to use a gun on nobody, no matter what. What do you think, Weasel?"

"Yeah," The Weasel said. "You may be right. You don't want to fool around with a dangerous thing like that, now do you, kid. If you'll just hand it over to—"

David was backing away, thinking desperately that he should have known better than to fool around with a gun, when the back door of Mr. Golanski's house opened with a bang. The light streamed out across the porch and framed in the doorway was a high shouldered, hulking figure. It was Mr. Golanski with his double-barrelled shotgun.

Chapter
Seventeen

"They're here! They're here, David. With a truck and everything." When Janie yelled, Esther and Blair got up off the floor where they'd been playing Chinese checkers and ran to join Janie and Amanda on the window seat. David followed more slowly. His breath had suddenly started to get quick and shallow the way it always did when he had to give an oral report in school.

In the driveway a man and woman were getting out of a blue car. Behind the car a big van was just coming to a stop. On the side of the van there was an oval shaped logo, a border of small "40"s surrounded a huge "TV". Channel 40 was the local TV station. David swallowed hard. "Okay, Blair," he said. "Don't forget." Blair went on staring out of the window. David pulled him off the window seat and turned him around. "What are we going to say if they mention a dog?" he prompted.

In a toneless chant—obviously reciting from memory—Blair said, "We're going to tell the truth, except about Nightmare. We're going to say it was just a stray dog, and he ran away."

"You probably won't have to say much," Amanda said. "David will do most of the talking. Just agree with what he says. Okay, Bleeper?"

"Okay," Blair said, "I remember."

"I wish they'd ask me," Janie said passionately. "I'd remember."

"How could you remember?" Esther said. "You weren't there."

"I know, stupid," Janie said. "What I remember is what they're supposed to say. I remember every bit of it. Most of it was my idea."

"David!" It was Dad, calling from downstairs.

"Okay, Blair," David said. "This is it."

In the living room the man and woman who'd gotten out of the car were standing near the mantel talking to Molly. On the other side of the room two other men were bustling around setting up lights and reflectors. Dad introduced everybody. The first man and woman were Mr. Gomez and Ms. Bell from the Valley Press, and the other two guys were from the TV station. Mr. Gomez was a newspaper photographer, and Ms. Bell was a reporter. It turned out she was the one who was going to ask the questions.

While they waited for the TV guys to get their lights ready, Mr. Gomez showed David and Blair where they were supposed to sit, in two chairs near the fireplace. Across the room Dad and Molly and the other kids were all lined up on the sofa, Dad and Molly at each end and Amanda and Esther in the middle. Janie was perched on the arm next to Dad, and he was hanging on to the back of her shirt. David hoped he didn't let go. If he did, she'd probably blast off from sheer excitement.

Except for the shallow breathing, David was feeling all right until the TV guys got their lights on and one of them picked up his camera. It was an enormous thing that sat on his shoulder, and when it turned its big round eye toward David, he suddenly felt like somebody was tightening a noose around his neck. For a panicky moment he was sure he wasn't going to be able to say a single word. If anyone had started counting down or warning him to get ready the way they do in the movies, he'd have cracked up for sure; but instead Ms. Bell just asked him a question in a normal tone of voice, and he managed to answer with a minor amount of stuttering and gulping.

"I understand you were in the woods looking for your little brother, when you came across the two escapees," she said. "Is that correct?"

"Yes," David said, "for Blair—I was looking. I mean, I found him first—before we found the two guys." He gulped, swallowed hard and tried again. "I found Blair, and we were starting home when we saw them. They were getting a drink from the lake."

"I see." Ms. Bell turned to Blair. "Were you frightened, Blair, when you saw the escaped prisoners?"

Blair smiled and tipped his head on one side. "Nooo," he said thoughtfully. "I wasn't."

Ms. Bell nearly fell off her chair with enthusiasm. Blair

had that effect on some people. "Really?" she said. "Why weren't you frightened?"

"I wasn't frightened because of . . ." Blair said and then suddenly he stopped. He put his hand over his mouth, and his eyes got very round.

"Blair!" Janie whispered loudly. "Because of the gun. Because of the gun." David kept his eyes on the camera. It was still pointing at him and Blair. There was the sound of Dad hushing Janie, and then Blair took his hand away from his mouth and went on. "Because of the gun," he said, nodding his head. Then he stopped saying anything. For several seconds the camera and Ms. Bell went on staring at Blair and Blair stared back, smiling calmly. At last Ms. Bell turned back to David.

"But Blair wasn't with you when you brought the prisoners to Mr. Golanski's farm?"

"Yes," David said, "I sent him home. After we got out of the hills, I sent him on home."

"Why did you do that?" Ms. Bell asked.

"To tell them I was coming. So they wouldn't worry."

Ms. Bell smiled. Turning to Dad she said, "And what did Blair tell you when he got home, Mr. Stanley?" The camera swiveled toward Dad.

Dad smiled. "His exact words were 'David says he'll be home as soon as he turns the prisoners over.' "

Everybody laughed. "I'm sure that eased your minds considerably," Ms. Bell said. "You must have been frantic."

"Yes," Dad said. "And we'd have been even more so if we'd realized how close to accurate Blair's account was. Blair does have a tendency to fantasize, and I must admit I wasn't entirely convinced that his prisoner story was based on fact. But we were worried, of course. We were just about to call the police when Mr. Golanski called to say that David had arrived at his farm with the two prisoners at gunpoint, and that the sheriff was there and all was well."

"Oh yes, about the gun." She turned back to David. "How did you happen to have a gun with you when you met the escapees?"

When the camera swung around, David immediately choked up again. "Who me?" he said stupidly. "How did we what? Oh—the gun. We found it in a cave. Actually Blair found it."

"And that's how you happened to be armed when you ran into the escaped convicts and were able to take them into custody?"

David swallowed hard. "Well, I had the gun then," he said, "but it wasn't any big deal. I didn't really do anything. They were both pretty sick."

"The convicts were sick?"

So David tried to explain how The Weasel had a bad dog bite, and Steve, the other one, had poison oak—and Ms. Bell laughed and said that didn't sound too life threatening, and she thought it was terribly brave of David to have captured two dangerous criminals single-handedly. Then she asked Dad and Molly some questions about how they felt about the whole thing, and Janie volunteered to tell how she felt, and then it was all over.

David supposed it could have been worse—but not much. Just as he'd feared, he'd tied up everytime he'd had to answer a question. The only good outcome, as far as he was concerned, was that there'd been no mention at all of a dog. He wondered about that—until later that day when two of the officers who'd been at Mr. Golanski's came to the house.

The sheriff's deputies had asked some questions the night before, but by Saturday afternoon they'd obviously thought of a lot more. This time most of their questions were about the gun, which they said was definitely the one that had been taken from the guard on the night of the escape. They wanted to know why the gun had been in the cave, why the convicts had left their only weapon there, and how David and Blair had happened to find it.

"Maybe it wasn't any good," David suggested. "Or maybe they were out of ammunition."

"It was operational and fully loaded," one of the policemen said.

"Oh," David said, and then—risking it—he asked cautiously, "What did they say? Why did they say they left it in the cave?"

The policeman grinned. "At this point they aren't saying anything," he said. "They're waiting to tell their lawyers."

So that explained it. Steve and Herbie hadn't mentioned Nightmare because they weren't talking about anything—at least not yet. But that didn't mean they wouldn't eventually. It was one more thing to worry about. And where Nightmare was concerned, it was only one of many.

In fact, it was only because of Nightmare that David hadn't been even more nervous about the TV interview beforehand, as well as more worried about the outcome afterwards. The thing was, he had too much else on his mind. Too much dog on his mind, actually.

When Blair had come home with Nightmare the night before, he'd done just as David told him and put Nightmare in the tool shed, where he'd stayed—for the time being. Later that night, when Amanda and Janie sneaked out to feed and water him, he was still there; but the next morning when David and Amanda had gone out very early, they'd found him wandering around the yard. He'd chewed the bandage off his foot, and the cut looked even more raw and puffy than it had the day before.

There had barely been time to get the foot cleaned and doctored and Nightmare coaxed back into the tool shed before Dad and Molly came down to breakfast. They'd had to leave him alone briefly during breakfast, but all the rest of the day, except at mealtimes and during the TV interview, they took turns keeping him company. On Saturday afternoon, Pete came over and helped out with the dog-sitting. But the whole situation was very nip and tuck, with several narrow escapes.

There were all kinds of dangerous possibilities. Neither Dad nor Molly had much interest in the tool shed, but there was always the chance they might decide to check it out, for some reason. Or Nightmare might wander out into the yard again during the day. Pete was repairing the door and the hole in the wall, but there was no telling whether Nightmare would scratch his way out again on Monday when they would have to shut him in while they were away at school. And then there was his foot. If it didn't start healing pretty soon, he would definitely have to be taken to a vet, and then the cat would be out of the bag for sure.

Late in the afternoon on Saturday they had a conference

about Nightmare's future. Dad and Molly had gone to a wine tasting party, and for the moment the coast was clear, so they brought Nightmare out of the tool shed. All six of them, including Pete, sat around on the lawn, with Nightmare sprawled happily in the center of the circle, and discussed his fate.

They all agreed that over the long run things didn't look good. In fact, at one point, Amanda even suggested giving up and telling Dad and Molly everything. David was amazed.

"We can't do that," he said.

"Look," she said, "don't you think that when they see him and hear about everything that's happened they'll weaken and let us keep him? I'll bet Mom will."

"It's not that," David said. "Dad probably would too. At least he might. But what he'd be sure to do is tell the authorities that we have him. He's got a real hang-up about notifying the proper authorities. And then they'll notify his ex-owner—who'll probably insist on having him shot."

"I bet you're right," Pete said to Amanda. "Davey's old man couldn't let them shoot the mutt, once he hears about how he helped catch the crooks and everything."

Amanda stared at Pete coldly. "What do you know about Davey's old man," she said. Pete didn't say anything more.

Then Tesser suggested that they should dye Nightmare black so his owner wouldn't recognize him—and Janie thought they all ought to run away and take him with them; but nobody came up with anything very practical. So they just went on as they had before—moment by moment—nip and tuck.

On Sunday, when the interview was to be shown on TV, Molly suggested going into town to some friends' house to watch. David declined with thanks. If they'd been able to get Channel 40 themselves—Westerly Road didn't have cable television—he might have watched it. But to sit around with some people he hardly knew and watch himself blowing it was not his idea of a good time.

Nobody understood it. Particularly Janie. Wild horses couldn't have kept Janie away from seeing herself on TV. They were all nagging at him all morning, and when Pete showed up and started nagging too, and promising to dog-sit while they were gone, David gave up and said he'd go. He really was curious to see just how bad it would be—and besides he had a plan.

When they were almost to town, he asked to be let off at the library instead. After another round of protests, Dad said for everyone to be still because David had the right to decide whether he wanted to see himself on TV or not.

When they pulled up in front of the library, David got out and waited until the station wagon had disappeared around the corner. Then he turned the other way and walked quickly down Main Street to the big Sears and Roebuck store. On the way to the second floor on the escalator, he put on his dark glasses and turned up his collar.

In the TV department a clerk was doing a hard-sell number for an overweight couple with two little overweight kids. David edged up to a TV set and turned it away from a 49er's football game—to something called *Local Color*, on Channel 40. But just as Ms. Bell came on, asking him the first question, the whole chubby family parked themselves between him and the screen. He moved to another set and got a glimpse of himself opening and shutting his mouth without saying anything, before another clerk came over and asked him if he needed any help. When he said no, the clerk switched the channel. By the time he finally found a set nobody else was interested in, Ms. Bell was interviewing Dad and Janie. Dad looked good, and Janie was obviously in her element. David went back to the library. It was probably just as well. He knew he wouldn't have liked it.

Chapter
Eighteen

If David thought at all about what was going to happen on Monday, it was only to hope that not very many people watched Channel 40 on a Sunday afternoon. Actually, he was fairly sure that nobody did, not in November anyway, when there was football on the major networks. But just in case someone had caught the "David Stanley Horror Show," he decided that the best defense would be to beat them to the draw by laughing at himself. "Yeah," he'd say, "I really got the collar on, didn't I. There goes my career as the next Dan Rather." It was a pretty good line, but he never got to use it.

It started out as soon as he and Amanda got on the bus. Everyone asked him questions and made a big fuss. Even Mr. Hobbs, the bus driver, who never said anything except "sit down" and "shut up," did a big number about welcoming

David on board and asking him if he'd been interviewed by *Time Magazine* yet. Then all the kids on the bus—even Amanda's friend Tammy and her brother—got into a scramble to see who could sit close enough to talk to him.

Nobody kidded him about choking up during the interview, in spite of the fact that it seemed like nearly everybody had seen it. And those who hadn't seen the TV program had read the story that had appeared in the *Valley Press*. All the way to school nobody talked about anything except how David had captured the escaped convicts. In fact, nobody talked much at all except David himself, because every time he stopped talking somebody asked another question. And that was just the beginning.

School was more of the same—a lot more. The principal called him "Our Local Hero" and made him stand up and take a bow during assembly. All day long whole gangs of people followed him around as if he were some kind of rock musician or movie star. And then, to top it all off, while he was waiting at the bus stop in the afternoon, a bunch of little kids came up and asked for his autograph. David A. Stanley's autograph! It was really weird.

One of the weirdest things about it was the way everybody seemed to be listening to him, but after a while he began to get the feeling that what he actually said didn't make any difference. What mattered wasn't what he'd done or hadn't done, but just the fact that he'd been in the papers and on TV. Right at first he kept saying that he hadn't really done anything, because the prisoners were so sick they were going to turn themselves in anyway. He said that in Mrs. Baldwin's class when she asked him to tell about his experience—and then she said that he was not only a hero but a modest hero, as well. So after a while he quit being modest, and everybody seemed to think that was all right, too.

But the really weirdest part was the way it made him feel. Right at first he'd been a little nervous—but not for long. Even before the morning was over, he quit worrying about what he was going to say because it was pretty obvious that whatever he said was going to be a big hit. By the end of the day, it was as if he were floating on a strange kind of high. He laughed and wised off and talked in a loud voice—and every once in a while he had a strange kind of disconnected feeling, as if he weren't really himself. As if the person who was doing all the talking and laughing had nothing to do with the real David Stanley. But it was still very exciting and a big kick. It was only later that a reaction set in.

When he first got home, Blair wanted him to go out and look at Nightmare's foot, and so he did. The swelling had gone way down, and the color was much more normal. While he was inspecting the paw and helping Blair put a new bandage on it, he started talking a little bit about what had happened at school, but Blair was all excited about how much better Nightmare's foot was and the fact that he hadn't tried to break out of the tool shed while they were all away at school. After a while David went back in the house to have some milk and cookies and got into a conversation with Amanda.

Amanda had seen what happened at the bus stop, but she didn't know anything about the rest of the day. So he told her about the assembly, and she kidded him about his grammar school groupies and the autograph thing. But then she started talking about a new guy in the tenth grade who'd just made it to the top of her "ten most" list—and how she'd bumped into him in the hall, "accidentally on purpose"— and how they'd talked for five or ten minutes afterwards —and how Eloise almost died of jealousy.

After Amanda went out, he went on sitting there at the kitchen table and thinking. The only cookies that were left were burnt on the bottom and tasted awful, and he'd begun to feel very depressed. He didn't know why—and he didn't really want to think about it. He just sat there for a while, poking black cookie crumbs around on the table cloth, and then Molly came in and asked him to take out the garbage. For some reason that was the last straw. He got up, grabbed the garbage and slammed out of the room. He could feel Molly's eyes staring after him in astonishment.

After he'd dumped the garbage, he climbed up into the tree house and just sat there feeling rotten. He didn't know why he'd had to take it out on Molly. In fact he didn't even know for sure what it was that was bugging him. Oh, he had a clue or two maybe, but he didn't feel like going into it. He was still sitting there in the tree house, with his chin on his knees, when he heard Pete clanking down the driveway on his antique bike.

"Ye gods," he said. "Just what I need."

But when Pete started yelling, "Dave. Hey, Davey," he stuck his head out of the window and answered.

"Hey. Whatcha doing up here all by yourself?" Pete said as he crawled into the tree house.

"I don't know," David said coldly. "What're you doing here?"

Pete's Expression-Number-Two: the Blank Stare, was blanker than usual. "I come up to see you."

"Oh yeah?" David was too depressed to be careful, or to care what might happen if he weren't. "You still looking for a chance to punch me out?"

Pete went on staring. "Punch you out? I'm not looking to punch you out."

David did a "big surprise" number. "You're not? Then what have you been hanging around for all this time?" He stared at Pete with grim satisfaction, while one interior voice told him that he was really asking for it, and another one answered that he didn't care. "Who cares?" he thought grimly staring straight back at Garvey. The stares locked and went on and on. "Blank stares at two paces," David thought and grinned, but Pete didn't grin back. Instead he dropped his eyes and started picking at a hole in the knee of his Levi's.

"Because of Amanda," he said.

For a minute David couldn't imagine what he was talking about. "What about Amanda?" he asked.

This time David's big surprise number was for real. Pete's expression was very un-Pete-like. Obviously David had been wrong about him only having two expressions. He had at least three, and this one looked miserable. "I come to see Amanda," he said. He went on poking at the hole in his knee. "She hates me, I guess. At least she acts like it. I dunno. You think she hates me, Davey?"

David was staring again, but this time it was with astonishment. Pete Garvey was in love with Amanda. He couldn't believe it. "You—er—like Amanda?" he asked.

Pete nodded. "Yeah," he said. "For a long time. Since we met out there in the woods that day."

"You mean—since she . . ." He didn't go on, but Pete did.

"Yeah. Since she . . ." He doubled up his fist and did a slow motion punch. Then he shook his head. "She sure has a great right hook." He sighed and went back to staring at his knees. "You think she hates me, Davey?"

"No. I don't think she hates you. In fact, she told me once that you were a real hunk?"

"Is that good?"

"Sure. She says that about Magnum and Burt Reynolds."

"Yeah?" Pete looked delighted.

"Of course, that was a long time ago. She's pretty changeable."

Pete nodded, looking miserable again.

"You know what?" David said. "I thought you were hanging around to get a chance to punch me out."

Pete frowned. "What for?"

"For getting you in trouble that day in Mrs. Baldwin's class."

Pete thought for quite a while before he said, "Oh that. I forgot about that a long time ago. Besides, I don't sneak around punching guys out in private. I usually don't bother unless people are watching."

"Why not?" David thought maybe he knew, but he wondered what Pete would say.

"I dunno." But then Pete sighed and said, "Yeah, I know. I like having people watch me do something I'm good at. I'm not good at much else."

"I'm no good at fighting," David said.

"Yeah," Pete said.

No one said anything more for quite a long while. David's depression returned with a vengeance. He felt lousy—and the reasons he was feeling lousy were poking long painful fingers out of the dark corners in his mind; then Pete opened his mouth and put another big clumsy finger right in the middle of the problem. Dead center.

"Hey," Pete said all of a sudden. "You're a real big shot. In the papers—on TV—a real hero."

He was grinning, chipped tooth and all, and for some reason it made David mad. "Big deal. I find a couple of half-dead escaped prisoners in the woods, and if anybody captures them it's Nightmare not me, and I get all the credit. Everybody talking about how brave I am and all that. I'm not." Speaking distinctly, pausing between every word, he went on, "I am not brave, and I know it. I've known it practically all my life."

"Hey, wait a minute," Pete said. "That's dumb. You're supposed to be a real smart guy, but that's the dumbest thing I ever heard. Just because you don't like to fight don't mean nothing. What about when we thought those crooks were outside your house and you went running out in the dark? And what about Friday when you went up in the hills all alone to look for Blair?"

"I was scared, that's what. I was scared to death."

"Yeah," Pete said, "that's what I mean. That's guts. That's real guts. Hell, Davey. You know what I think. I think nobody's got more real guts than you."

At first David just said, "Oh sure," and laughed sarcastically; but the more he thought about what Pete said, the more sense it made, and the better it made him feel. He was just about to tell Pete so, when they heard Molly calling. Pete rattled off on his bike, and David went on in to have dinner and answer a lot more questions about his big day at school. It was no big deal.

Chapter
Nineteen

After dinner that night *David Copperfield* was on television, and everybody watched. At least, everyone was in the room for quite a long while. Blair was sitting next to David on the couch, and he did seem to be pretty restless, but David thought it was just because Dickens was a little over his head. Finally he got up and went out of the room. Right after that the movie got more interesting—it was the part where David Copperfield runs away from London—and nobody thought about Blair's absence. It wasn't until the next commercial that Molly suddenly asked where he was.

"He went out," David said. "I think he—" He was about to say that Blair had probably gone up to bed, when he happened to look toward the hall and the words froze in his throat. Blair was standing in the door to the hall, and Nightmare was with him. Blair was smiling and holding onto

Nightmare's collar. On the dog's huge bristly head—exactly level with Blair's curly blond one—the floppy ears were tilted forward in their alert position. He looked tense and watchful and—even when you were used to him—incredibly enormous.

David started shaking his head and making "go away" gestures, but he was too late. Molly, who was sitting on the floor leaning against Dad's legs, saw what David was doing and leaned out around Dad's chair. "Saints in heaven!" she said in a high, thin voice.

Dad looked around and jumped to his feet. Then everybody was jumping up and running in all directions. David was trying to get in between Dad and Nightmare, Molly was trying to get to Blair, and most of the other kids were trying to stop her. David yelled, "Get him out of here, Blair," and Dad yelled, "Blair, come here." Everybody else seemed to be yelling something; and to make matters worse, Nightmare started to bark. The yelling and barking and pushing and pulling seemed to go on for a long time before it suddenly got quiet. It ended with David standing in front of Dad with his arms stretched out as if he were trying to block a pass, and Esther and Janie and Amanda all holding onto Molly. Blair and Nightmare were still standing in the doorway.

The quiet lasted for several seconds, and then Dad said, "My God, Blair. What is that enormous creature?"

"My dog," Blair said. "This is my dog."

There was another long silence, and then Molly began to giggle. "It's his dog. His dog, Jeff. Blair's imaginary dog."

She laughed harder, and after a minute Dad began to laugh, too. They stopped laughing once and looked at each other and started all over again. When they finally stopped laughing, Dad looked at Blair and Nightmare and shook his head slowly, as if he still couldn't quite believe his eyes. "Son," he said, "is this the dog you've been talking about? The one that was lost last week?"

"Yes," Blair said. "We found him again. His name is Nightmare."

"I can well believe it," Dad said. "Well, bring him on in and let's get acquainted."

"Wait a minute," David said. "Nightmare is nervous about men. You'd better let him get used to you a little first."

Dad looked at David sharply. "You knew about this?" he asked.

David swallowed hard. But before he could think of a good way to start explaining, Molly interrupted. "Will he let me pat him, Blair?" Then she giggled again and said, "Will your imaginary dog let me pat him?"

"I'll tell him," Blair said. He put his hands on each side of Nightmare's face and pulled his head around and whispered in his ear. After a minute he smiled at Molly. "Okay," he said. "It's okay, now."

Molly went up to Nightmare then, moving slowly and talking in a soothing voice. As soon as he'd sniffed her hand, he began to wag his tail. It took a little more time with Dad. When he began to move forward, Nightmare growled softly; it was only after Dad squatted down and talked to him softly for several minutes that he stopped growling and let him get closer. Everyone stood around and watched and told Nightmare what a good dog he was, and at last he let Dad scratch behind his ears, while the little kids crowded around and patted him, too.

When the introductions were finally over, Nightmare trotted over in front of the fireplace and flopped down on the rug. He put his chin on his front paws and rolled his eyes around, looking from one person to another. Then he sighed a tremendous sigh and thumped his tail twice on the floor. Everybody laughed.

"Okay," Dad said, when they'd stopped laughing, "now how about some explanations?" He was smiling, but his tone of voice made it obvious that he meant business.

"I'll explain," Janie said. "I can explain everything."

"Fine," Dad said, "but I think we'll start with Blair. After all, he's got some catching up to do. He's been trying to tell us about this dog for a long time, and I haven't been listening. Where did he come from, Blair?"

Blair went over and sat down beside Nightmare on the rug. "He came from the hill," he said, "at night. At night he came and sat in the garden, and I went down to see him. And I fed him, and then he went away. And then I told Janie and Esther, and they fed him, too. And then David and Amanda and Pete found out, and they helped, too. And—and—that's all."

"That's all?" Dad said.

"Dad," Janie interrupted. "Do I get an extra week's allowance, now? Because I didn't really do what you told us not to. You said not to talk to Blair about imaginary dogs, and . . ."

"I get your point," Dad said. "Okay, Janie. Not guilty

on that particular charge. But how about what I said about no more pets. I'm afraid you've all been more than a little guilty on that particular ruling. You all agreed—no more pets, and then you all apparently entered into a conspiracy to adopt a dog and keep it a secret from Molly and me."

It suddenly got very quiet. With a sinking sensation David remembered his own predictions about what Dad would say and do if he found out about Nightmare. What was Blair thinking of, to drag Nightmare right into the house in front of everybody? And just when things were going so well, too, with Nightmare learning to stay in the tool shed and his foot beginning to heal up. And now Dad was going to start with all the logical and reasonable reasons why Nightmare wouldn't be able to stay. "Wait 'til I get him alone," David thought. "Just wait 'til I get Blair alone."

It was Amanda who broke the silence first. "Okay. We are guilty, I guess. All of us. But before you and Mom start handing out judgments, I think you ought to hear the whole story. Like for instance, how Nightmare was with David and Blair when they bumped into those guys in the woods—and what might have happened to them if he hadn't been, and how . . ."

"Wait a minute. Wait a minute," Dad said. "David? What's this about—the prisoners?"

"Well," David said. "I guess it would be better if we started at the beginning."

So they did. First David told how it had all started with Blair going out alone to feed and play with Nightmare at night—when everyone thought he was just walking in his sleep. And then how Esther and Janie got in on the act, and the stormy night when he and Amanda and Pete discovered what was going on. Molly was amazed when he told about Nightmare hiding in the closet with Blair the night she came to the room. "I can't believe it," she kept saying. "That monster was really right there in the closet that night. I can't believe it."

When he started on what they'd found out about Nightmare's history, Janie interrupted and said that since she'd found out about it, she ought to be the one that got to tell it. So she did, in great detail, and when she got to the part about Sam Plenty and how he'd tried to make a killer out of Nightmare and then took him out in the woods and shot him, Molly said, "How terrible! What a dreadful man. The poor dog." When she said "poor dog," Nightmare did his mournful eyebrows number and wagged his tail, and she got up and went over to him and petted him and called Dad over to feel the scar that ran across the side of his head.

David took over again then and told about the capture of the criminals. He tried not to leave anything out, and when he did, one of the other kids would remind him. The whole thing took a long time. He was only about halfway through when Esther said she was hungry, and everybody took time out to go into the kitchen and get cookies and milk. Nightmare went along too, and the little kids gave him bites of cookie and showed Dad and Molly how carefully he took food from your fingers, without biting off your whole hand, like he could have done easily if he'd wanted to.

David really began to hope when he saw Dad sneaking Nightmare a bite of his cookie on the way back into the living room. He wasn't sure, though, not even when Dad sent

Janie to his study for his first aid kit and changed the bandage on Nightmare's foot himself.

When he'd finally finished, and all Dad and Molly's questions had been answered, it suddenly got very quiet. Everyone was looking at Dad. Dad was looking at Molly. "Molly," he said, "most of the burden would be on you."

Molly was smiling. "How could an imaginary dog be a burden?"

Dad grinned. "But a pet is time consuming—even the best behaved . . ."

Molly got up off the floor and sat in Dad's lap. "Jeff," she said, "checking to see that all the doors are locked after you've all gone off to school is time consuming. Worrying about funny noises when I'm here alone is time consuming. Nightmare's going to save me a lot of time."

"Right," Dad said, and everybody cheered. Nightmare's head came up off his paws, and he wagged his tail.

"Just a minute, now," Dad said. "We will have to check with the authorities. There may be problems."

"Daddy," Esther whimpered.

"But, I imagine we can solve them," Dad said.

David was sure that they could.

Chapter
Twenty

David couldn't get to sleep. Across the room Blair was curled up in one corner of his bed, and Nightmare was stretched out across most of the rest of it. David turned and flopped and unwound himself from the covers—and then wound himself up again. Finally he got up and, taking a blanket with him, he went to sit on the window seat. Wrapping himself in the blanket, he stared down into the silent moon-shadowed garden.

He didn't know why he couldn't sleep. Normally when he had insomnia, it was because he was worried about something, and tonight he wasn't. For the first time in quite a while there was nothing concerning Nightmare to worry him, but that wasn't all. A bunch of other stuff that used to keep him awake nights had suddenly disappeared, or turned into something a lot different.

That was it, really he decided. A lot of things suddenly looked different. It seemed as if people just naturally got locked into seeing their problems in a certain way, until after a while they forgot that there was any other way to look at them. When actually, they might not seem like problems at all if they were looked at from a slightly different angle.

Like, Dad and Molly, for instance and their quarrel over whether Blair ought to have an imaginary dog. If they hadn't been looking at their quarrel so hard, they'd have probably had time to ask Blair a few more questions and find out what was really worrying him.

And Dad and Molly weren't the only ones. There were several things that David was suddenly seeing from another perspective. Like how Amanda really felt about him—and how Jeff and Molly really felt about each other—and most surprising, perhaps, the whole Pete thing. How Pete felt about David—and how David felt about Pete. He'd been so sure for all those weeks that Pete was only interested in punching him out. He'd been so sure that Pete was nothing but a stupid bully. Pete was certainly a bully at times, and he might not be the brightest guy in the world about some things. But it was Pete who'd told him something very important about himself—and about courage. And now, because of Pete, he was pretty sure he was finished with one particular hang up—because, as Pete said, there were lots of different ways of having guts, and some of them weren't as important as others.

David was still staring out the window and thinking when he heard Blair say "Hi." He turned around in time to see Blair climbing over Nightmare. Nightmare looked up and wagged his tail and went back to sleep, and Blair crawled up on the window seat beside David. David put one end of his blanket around him, and they both sat there for a while looking out at the darkness. David was trying to think of a way to explain what he'd been thinking about to Blair.

"It's getting locked into seeing something in a certain way," he told Blair, "until you can't see any other possibilities. It's a matter of point of view. Do you know what I mean?"

Blair stared at him. "Nooo," he said.

"Well, like—like I was so sure that Dad would make us get rid of Nightmare if he found out. You know, he doesn't change his mind very often, and I was sure he'd never change it about a dog." He laughed, and Blair laughed too. "I was really P.O.ed at you for bringing him in the house tonight. At first, I mean. I was sure you'd really blown it for poor old Nightmare."

"Are you P.O.ed at me now?" Blair asked.

"No. Of course not. Everything turned out great. But it might not have, you know. I mean, deciding to bring Nightmare in like that, without telling anybody what you were going to do. You were really taking a big chance."

Blair didn't say anything. It was hard to tell in the dim light, but suddenly David was sure he was smiling.

"Blair! You didn't know, did you? Did you know how things were going to turn out?"

Blair shook his head. "No," he said. "But Harriette did."

David sighed. "Blair. There's no such person as . . ." But then he stopped. Having a friend like Harriette, like a lot of other things, was probably all a matter of point of view.

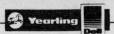

Masterful mysteries
by
PHYLLIS REYNOLDS NAYLOR

(Winner of the Edgar Allan Poe Award)